MW01480801

First Encounter

Connie Cockrell

DEDICATION

To the family and friends, too numerous to mention, that have encouraged me along the path to author hood.

ACKNOWLEDGMENTS

To Randy Cockrell for the final line editing. To my friends at Forward Motion (http://www.fmwriters.com), Holly Lisle's How To Think Sideways (https://howtothinksideways.com/login/), and Power Writing Hour for their support.. To the wonderful editors at Silver Jay Media for helping me make this work as good as it could be.

THEY LEAVE THE SCHOOL

Alyssa stared out of the front door of the Catholic school where she'd been born. It was an industrial-looking building, built in 1961, and it had been a designated Civil Defense shelter since it was finished. In front of her was the old front lawn, now turned into a garden. It was over three acres of green growing things, the first time in just over seventeen years that the earth had clean soil and the ability to grow anything other than stunted, poisoned life.

Kyra saw her friend Alyssa standing there waiting for her, but she had one more goodbye to make. The community leader, Malcolm Smith, stood near her in the atrium of the school's front entry. At six foot one, Malcolm stood a whole head taller than Kyra. The Mother Superior was next to him. The nuns had supplied the school as their shelter all those years ago. Kyra and Alyssa had already said goodbye to her and the rest of the community at breakfast. She stood, fingering the beads of her rosary, whispering her prayers for their safe travels.

Kyra gave Malcolm a hug. His eyebrows shot up. Kyra wasn't one for hugging. "Don't be a sissy," she told him when she let him go. "I owe you, more than just a hug."

His close-cropped wooly hair was nearly pure white. He'd been the leader in this school building, a refuge from the toxic brown rain that began seventeen years ago and didn't stop for four years, from the beginning. His dark brown skin was wrinkled now, worry creasing his eyes. Kyra did her best to memorize his face. "If it wasn't for you, I wouldn't be able to take this journey."

"Don't go, Kyra. Talk Alyssa into staying. She can heal the earth

1

from here, a base camp, circling out all the time."

She adjusted her pack straps. "I tried that, Malcolm. I've been trying to talk her out of this for over a year. She says she has to go. The planet is calling to her."

His mouth twisted. "You believe her?"

Kyra stopped fussing with her pack and looked him in the eye. "You know what she can do. None of the rest of us can do that. So, yeah. I believe her." Kyra's grey-blue eyes became determined. "She says she has to go. I have to go with her. Who else will protect her?"

Malcolm shrugged. "Just you. I shouldn't be surprised. She's been your special project since you were four. We'll miss you both." He clapped her on both shoulders "We'll miss you."

She took a deep breath. "Take care, Malcolm." She turned away and stopped at the door where she picked up a quiver full of arrows the community had recovered for her from a nearby hunting store and slung it over her shoulder. Then she grabbed her bow, string loosened. "I'm ready, Alyssa."

The sun was shining from a clear blue sky, making the seventeen-year-old's nearly white blond hair glow in the light. She wore it loose and it fell around her shoulders in a smooth flow to the middle of her back. A light breeze caused wisps of hair to float around her face. She smiled. "It's a good day to start, Kyra." She walked out the door and past the overhang into the garden.

Kyra pulled her waist-length braid of medium brown hair over her shoulder--the pack was pulling on it, and followed her friend. They passed several people they knew in the gardens, who stopped weeding and other chores to wave when the two women passed by.

It didn't take long to walk through the acres around the school that Alyssa had already cleared for their community in Midland, Pennsylvania. There was plenty of space for more gardens, even some livestock if they should find a surviving pig or goat or chickens. The teams had been looking since Alyssa had started to clear the land. So far they hadn't found any.

They were headed west to the other side of Midland where there would be a stream. Alyssa had chosen the direction. Kyra had wanted to go east, toward the sea. "It's important we go west," Alyssa had told her friend.

"Why?" Kyra asked as they stood in a classroom in front of a map of the United States, pulled down in front of the chalkboard.

Alyssa stared at the mountains, rivers and valleys in browns and blues and greens drawn on the map. "I'm needed to the west." She looked at her friend. "We're needed to the west."

Kyra shrugged. "Fine," she conceded. "West it is."

They stopped as they reached the edge of the brown. That's what Kyra called it. It was the remains of the toxic brown rain that covered everything and unless people wore protective gear, they had to remain in place. It had kept them trapped in the school for seventeen years. Under it, plants grew but they were sickly and stunted. Alyssa bent over and touched the oily brown slime, passing her hand over it in a swath. The slime dissolved, the plants turned from a nasty yellow-green to a more healthy green and began to stand up in the sunlight.

Kyra watched for only a moment. She'd been with Alyssa as she cleared the school grounds and had seen the process before. Now, she kept an eye on the path they wanted to take, steering Alyssa left or right as needed. As Alyssa cleaned a four-foot-wide area, Kyra looked for animals. She'd seen things slinking through the ailing woods, just out of sight.

At first she didn't believe it. Malcolm hadn't either when she'd told him about the sightings. "Can't be," he'd said. "You were just four. The rain killed just about everything it touched when it came. That's why there are so few of us left. How can animals have lived all these years out there in the poison?"

She had merely shrugged. She didn't have any answer but she knew there were things out there and that they'd be hungry.

At mid-day she made Alyssa stop. Kyra poured some of their precious water over Alyssa's hands to clean them. Then they sat down to eat. Kyra had the provisions, the tent and her own gear. Alyssa carried her own sleeping bag, extra clothing, her water bottle and the few personal items she decided to bring. They sat with backs against the packs as Kyra passed her a bean cake and cut-up carrots.

The school had seeds, part of the Civil Defense provisions. What they didn't have were animals. The nuns hadn't even kept chickens. Since the school survived on grow-beds inside the school, next to all of the west and south-facing windows, their diet had been vegetarian. Beans were the primary form of protein. Alyssa ate in silence.

"I think we've come about two miles, Alyssa."

The pale young woman nodded. She never tanned, no matter how much sunlight hit her skin. "It's the woods. It takes longer to heal them than the open grassland around the school. It takes more energy, too."

Kyra held her hand vertically, palm away from her, and moved it until the lower edge of her thumb lined up with what horizon she could see. The sun was five hand-widths above the horizon. "Only about five hours of daylight left."

"I'll do what I can," Alyssa replied and closed her eyes.

Kyra let her nap and leaned back against a tree. Alyssa had been right this morning at the school door. It was a good day for travelling. The sky was a clear, cornflower blue on a fine mid-May day. Occasional puffy white clouds drifted overhead while a slight breeze kept it from being too hot.

Despite Malcolm's doubts, today Kyra had seen the occasional bug flying by and even ants under the dense cover of trees. *It's too bad the Brown smells bad,* she thought as she looked over at Alyssa napping. It wasn't an overpowering smell, just a lingering odor of rancid oil or medicine always in the background.

Her head snapped up at the sound of birdsong. Overhead, against the blue sky, she saw the silhouette of a bird. Her heart quickened and a smile crossed her face. "I told you, Malcolm," she whispered. She let Alyssa sleep for half a hand, then woke her up. "We need to get going or we won't have any water tonight."

Alyssa nodded, rose and put her pack back on. She worked, swinging her hands back and forth across the path, four inches at a time. The two were going around the town. They decided it made no sense to clear the asphalt and cement of Midland more than she had already done. That work had allowed the members of the community access to the town for any remaining supplies.

It took time to heal the woods. Kyra made her stop once an hour to drink, holding the bottle for her so they wouldn't waste any cleaning her hands. When the sun set, Kyra dug the hand-drawn map she'd copied from the school room map of the local area out of her pack. In the fading light she studied the terrain around her, using her compass to check directions. She sighed.

"Alyssa, stop. We're not going to get to the stream tonight. It's getting too dark to see and it's probably another mile. We'll stop here for the night."

Alyssa stood up and stretched her arms up and over her head.

"Okay." She looked around. They had stopped in a small glade, wilted trees surrounding a somewhat flat area. "I can clear this a bit so we have a place to pitch the tent."

After half an hour she had an area cleared big enough to pitch the tent and an additional area so they had a place to relieve themselves without stumbling into the oily brown slime by accident. At the edge of the clearing, Kyra used more water to clean Alyssa's hands. There was half a bottle left. Alyssa spread her bag inside the tent next to Kyra's and lay down.

"You need to eat," Kyra said as she handed Alyssa another bean cake.

She sat up and slowly ate, taking just a few sips of water after it was gone to wash it down. She lay back on the bag. "I'm sorry I couldn't get us to the stream."

"Don't worry about it," Kyra said. She hiccupped, the dry bean cake stuck in her throat. She took a small swallow of water, simply so she wouldn't choke on her food. One more sip followed the last bite of the cake. The rest of the water would make oatmeal for them in the morning. "We'll get there tomorrow."

In the morning Kyra woke first. Dew had fallen in the night and she used her bandana to wipe it off of the now healed grasses. She wrung it into the water bottles, then sucked on the bandana for what moisture she could get. By the time Alyssa woke, the oatmeal was cooked. Kyra handed her a spoon. The two of them ate out of the small pot.

"How are you?" Kyra asked as she scrubbed the pot with grass.

"Tired. But I can get us to the stream and clean some water."

"Good," Kyra said as she packed the pot away.

They packed their sleeping bags and the tent and hefted packs. Kyra made sure the tiny fire she made to cook breakfast was put out.

Alyssa went back to her stopping point and began to heal. The spring morning was warm and it got warmer as the morning wore on. It was noon before they reached the stream where she collapsed in a heap after clearing space right to the water's edge. Kyra gave her the rest of the water, no more than a cup. "Come on, Alyssa. I'll let you rest while I prep the spot. Then you need to clean the water."

This had been a major sticking point in their plans. Alyssa knew she could clean the water but water flows along. As soon as she healed the area around her hand, it was washed away by more toxic water. Collecting rain water was one solution. It came down clean, only contaminated upon hitting the earth. But it didn't rain every day. Some other method had to be found.

After weeks of trial and error on the stream that came from the spring at the school, they decided on just scooping it into a pot and she'd clean that, water, pot and all. It took time but it was the simplest solution.

Kyra pulled the pot from her pack and scooped up water from the small stream. The pot and the surface of the water were covered in a thin brown slime. She held the pot by the handle, which she had carefully kept out of the water, and carried it to Alyssa.

Alyssa sat up and ran her hands over the pot and then in the water. The slime disappeared. Kyra wondered again where the slime went. Did it go into Alyssa? Did she change it chemically? She'd asked Alyssa a few months after they knew she could heal the brown rain slime.

"I don't know," then thirteen-year-old Alyssa had said when asked the first time. She knelt over the tiny spot of grass she'd healed just out from under the edge of the pavilion that covered the spring the convent school was famous for. "I can see the grass, just like I can see the plants in the grow-beds inside. I can see what's wrong with them and make it right."

Seventeen-year-old Kyra had stood under the pavilion. She didn't want to touch the brown slime. "How do you know what's right?"

Alyssa had turned her head from the grass to Kyra and blinked. "I just know. It feels right."

Now, after the water was clean, Kyra poured it into the water bottles. She made six trips before the bottles were full, then made one more trip. "To clean up with," she told her friend. They cleaned Alyssa's hands with bandanas specifically for the purpose, then wiped down faces and bodies. "That feels better," Alyssa said. "I already miss the showers at the school, even if they were cold."

They drank their fill and decided to camp next to the stream. "It's harder than I thought," Alyssa said. "The acres around the school were easier."

"We'll get the hang of it," Kyra said as she set up the tent. "We have all the time in the world."

Alyssa nodded, but her eyes said something else.

THE ANIMALS REVEAL THEMSELVES

Every day was much like the first. Nearly two decades of growth, even as stunted and sickly as it was, made the going difficult. Kyra revised her plan of five or more miles a day. Alyssa couldn't heal that fast. They inched along and the first few days Kyra was hyper-alert. Every sound was new and regarded as a potential threat. By the end of the day she was as exhausted as Alyssa.

After she became accustomed to the noises and eventually identified what made them, she began to relax. To keep her mind occupied she asked Alyssa about the plants she healed. "Can we eat any of this stuff?"

Alyssa stopped and stretched. She pointed at a small bunch of three-leafed plants that grew close to the ground. "That's wood sorrel. It has a nice citrus tang. It's good in salads and has a lot of vitamin C but it also has a lot of oxalate and can cause stomach cramps if too much is eaten." She grinned at Kyra. "It makes a nice tea, too. You can pick some if you like and taste it and bring a few stems with us. It would be nice to have a tea with supper tonight."

Kyra arched an eyebrow and regarded her friend. "You're not kidding? We can eat that?"

Alyssa nodded. "I know. It's a little strange to eat wild food after growing up in a shelter our whole lives, but I'm sure. We can eat it. Pick a sprig for me, would you?"

Kyra was unsure of this whole thing. Eat wild food? But Alyssa said it was okay. She sighed and stepped over to the three-inch-tall plants. The leaves were split into threes, a shamrock- looking plant.

She picked two stems and stood up. Alyssa opened her mouth and Kyra put a stem and leaves on her tongue. She watched as her friend chewed, her eyes closed.

Alyssa swallowed and opened her eyes. "So that's what lemon tastes like." She glanced at the stem still in Kyra's hand. "You try it."

Kyra's lips pressed together as she held the stem between two fingers. She stared at Alyssa. Her friend laughed. "Go ahead, it's good."

With a sigh, Kyra put the plant in her mouth. The first sensation was of coolness; then she got the flavor of green, growing things. She chewed. The tender green stem crunched lightly between her teeth and a tart, slightly sour flavor flooded her mouth. It was such a surprise that she almost spit it out but Alyssa was watching, a grin on her face. Kyra chewed some more and swallowed.

"What do you think?"

"I think that much flavor is a big surprise, but good. How'd you know so much about it?"

Alyssa turned and began healing again. "From the plant books in the school library. There were a lot of books in there about wild and domestic plants. I memorized all of it."

"Pretty cool, Alyssa." Kyra picked a few stems and tucked them into a pocket. "Speaking of food, it's been five days and I haven't found any animal we can eat. We'll need to divert into a town and try to find some food."

"Fair enough. Tell me which way to go and I'll get us there."

Kyra took out her map and studied it as Alyssa inched forward. Figuring four miles per day, they'd come about twenty miles. She looked at her map with the compass on top of it. They were heading in a north-west direction. A town was nearby but she understood they weren't traveling in a straight line. There was a stream about two miles away; she'd head for that and with luck they'd be there by nightfall.

"Looks like a town is nearby, maybe two days away. I'll show you on the map when we stop for the night. "

"Sounds good, Kyra."

#

Two days later they stood on a hill overlooking a small town, called Station Mills, on the map. "It doesn't look like much does it?" Alyssa said.

Kyra shook her head. Some of the buildings had collapsed, age and snow damage, she thought. The main part of town looked intact. She hoped a grocery store would be on their path. "No sign of any survivors."

Alyssa shrugged. "Hard to tell. They'd be staying inside, the same way we did." She pointed. "That looks like a grocery, there on the edge of town."

Kyra looked where her friend was pointing. "Yeah, let's head toward that. If it doesn't work out, we'll head into town to see what we can find."

It took the rest of the day for Alyssa to clear a path to the building. "Yes!" Kyra exclaimed when they reached the front of it. "Greenway" was written in fading formed letters over the front door, the "A" hanging crookedly into the "W." Alyssa cleaned the old-fashioned door so Kyra could touch it. Kyra grabbed the rusting vertical hand-bar and pulled. It didn't open. She pulled harder. Still nothing.

"Maybe the other side," Alyssa suggested.

Kyra nodded and grabbed the bar on the left door. It creaked. "Must be rusted shut." She took her pack off and, with one foot against the right hand door, pulled as hard as she could. The door screamed in protest as it opened four inches, leaving a rust trail on the cement under it. She grinned. "Let's see if I can get it open a little more."

She braced her back against the right hand door and shoved hard. The door screamed some more as it opened wider. "That should do it." She slapped her hands together to get rid of the dirt. "Let's see what the good people of Station Mills have left for us."

She slung her pack over a shoulder and went in, Alyssa following. "I talked to Malcolm about this before we left," she said over her shoulder. "Canned goods are off limits. After all this time, even if the cans haven't exploded with botulism, they're not safe to eat. We're looking for dry goods; pasta, rice, beans, cereal, anything like that."

"I've always wanted to try pasta," Alyssa said. "The cookbooks and stories make it sound wonderful."

Kyra studied the signs over the aisles. "Here, let's try this aisle."

As they turned, they could see the remains of plastic bags and boxes all over the floor. Three steps into the aisle, a rat squeaked and jumped off of a shelf in front of them. Alyssa gave a little shriek and jumped aside. Kyra stood wide-eyed and frozen in the middle of the aisle. "That was a rat!" She turned to her friend. "Did it look sickly to you?"

Alyssa swallowed and shook her head. "No, it looked healthy."

"Rats can be eaten," Kyra said quietly. "It looks like quite a few have been using this place as their pantry. Let's see if they left us anything." They searched the shelves, Alyssa simply looking because they hadn't cleaned her hands before they came inside. Rat droppings were everywhere, as were empty boxes and bags. They saw the occasional rat and the rare mouse scurry ahead of them through the store. They searched all of the aisles only to find more trash.

"Maybe in the back. The store might have had a shipment but never got it on the shelves," Kyra said. They headed to the back and Kyra slowly pushed open the swinging door. Rats went running in every direction.

Alyssa wrinkled her nose. "It smells in here."

Kyra held a hand over her face. "Yeah," she said as she took a shallow breath. "It stinks. Stay here and hold the door open. I'll do a quick search of the pallets." The storage area ran the width of the store. She checked the closest pallet. "It says it's macaroni and cheese," she called out. Kyra pulled broken boxes away from the torn plastic wrapping the pallet. Rodent droppings showered to the floor. "Hah!" she crowed. She held up an undamaged box. "The rats haven't gotten to the center of the pallet. We've got food!"

She grabbed four boxes and moved to the next pallet, which was labeled "Rice Dinner." She pulled a few more boxes from the center and stuffed them into her pack. By the time she finished, she also had dried milk, oatmeal and Ramen in her pack. "I got enough for a week," she said as she approached the door. "I even found tea bags, though I'm not sure how good they'll be after all this time."

Alyssa nodded. "If they're spoiled, we'll just dump them. Let's get out of here, I can't breathe."

Dinner that night was in the town park, next to the creek marked "Mills Creek", on the map. Alyssa cleaned enough water for them to wash, drink and make one of the macaroni and cheese dinners. "Pretty good," Kyra said, "even though we didn't have any butter to add to it."

"I can see why there were so many recipes for pasta in the cookbooks." Alyssa licked her spoon. "Very good."

"I'm wondering if I should try to catch some rat," Kyra said as she scrubbed the pot out with clean grass.

"We don't need it yet, Kyra." Alyssa became serious, her green eyes narrowed and her lips pressed together. "I'd hate for us to kill anything if we have plenty of food."

Kyra chewed her lip. While she was eager to try out the skills Malcolm had taught her, she was anxious about the idea of killing an animal and then having to gut and skin it. "Later then."

#

The pair was outside their second town, two weeks after leaving their home in Midland. They'd just resupplied as they had in Station Mills. They were feeling pretty good. Alyssa was developing her stamina and they were moving along at five miles a day. Kyra was confident. They were healthy, moving along at a good pace and eating well. She'd seen some animals lurking in the woods but nothing came into clear sight. She didn't want to try to shoot an arrow at whatever it was, then spend time retrieving the arrow. She felt as long as it didn't bother them, she wouldn't bother it.

That evening Kyra built a small fire to cook over and was getting the pot and water ready when Alyssa said quietly, "There's a dog behind you."

Kyra froze. Her bow was behind her, strung tight and leaning against her pack but it was out of reach. "How far away?" she whispered.

"The edge of the clearing, about twenty feet." Her eyes were wide and Kyra could see her friend swallow. "It's a big dog, Kyra."

"Does it look sick?"

Alyssa shook her head a little. "It's not fat but it looks strong."

"Crap." She forced herself to stand up slowly. Her knees popped as they straightened. "What's the dog doing?"

"It's sniffing the air."

"It didn't move?"

"No, it's still at the edge of the woods."

Kyra casually turned. Now she could see the dog. She tried not to look at it as she took the three steps to her pack. The quiver was next to it. She put the quiver on in long slow movements and picked up her bow. When she looked again, there were three dogs, spread in a line at the edge of the clearing. "Alyssa, do you have your knife in your boot?"

"Yes," the young woman whispered.

"Stand up slowly and as you stand, pull your knife. Don't make any sudden or sharp movements."

Kyra watched the dogs as she nocked the arrow in the bow. "Are you standing?"

"Yes."

Kyra's stomach rolled and her heart was beating so fast she thought she would be sick. She swallowed and made an effort to breathe in slow, even breaths. "Stay behind me as best you can. If one of the dogs gets past me, you'll have to kill it before it kills you. Understand?"

"I understand," Alyssa said in a weak voice.

The first dog, what looked like a German shepherd to Kyra, began to circle the small camp to her right, its lip curled and wicked teeth visible in the fading light. A second dog circled to the left. Kyra felt her hands begin to sweat. She pulled the bow and held it. Maybe they'll go away, she thought.

The third dog approached straight into the camp, directly toward Kyra. She glanced at the first dog, it was still circling. "Alyssa, keep an eye on the dog to our left. Let me know if he charges, I can't watch all three of them at once."

"Yeah," she whispered.

Kyra held her shot. Now that it had come down to it, she was reluctant to kill the dog. She was reluctant to kill anything. She'd only shot at targets back at the school. Malcolm had told her not to hesitate.

"The first time is going to be hard, Kyra," he'd told her. A faraway look shone in his eyes. "It will be the hardest thing you've ever done, but if you're threatened, don't hesitate. Doesn't matter if it's an animal or a human. Hesitation will get you and Alyssa killed. Take the shot."

Sweat ran down her forehead and into the outer corner of her left eye. She blinked and the center dog, crouched down, approached slowly. The first dog was on her right, also in a crouch. "Alyssa, is your dog in a crouch?"

"Yes. I think it's going to attack."

"I think so, too." Kyra pulled the string back just a hair more and fired at the center dog. The dog screamed and flipped around as the arrow hit it in the middle of its chest. She turned to her right and pulled a new arrow in one fluid movement. The first dog was charging. She could hear Alyssa scream, "Look out!" behind her. The first dog was five feet away when Kyra pulled the bow and shot it in the neck. She dropped the bow and pulled her boot knife while spinning around to Alyssa. The last dog was in the air, a snarl sounding as it leapt straight for Alyssa's face.

Kyra threw her knife and hit the dog in the ribs, knocking it aside. It yelped and rolled. Kyra grabbed the knife from Alyssa, who stood frozen, and charged the dog. It rolled to its feet with a yelp and crouched, ready to lunge. All she could see was its mouth in a snarl and teeth ready to tear her apart. The blood pounded in her ears as she circled the dog. The thing must weigh about fifty pounds, she thought as she gripped Alyssa's knife. *It's wounded. I can do this.*

It leapt, her knife falling out of its ribs. She braced herself in a crouch for the impact. Kyra slashed with the knife at the animal's throat but it wasn't enough. It yowled as she spun to get out of its way. She crouched again, knife ready as the dog hit the ground, spun around and leapt at her again. This time she let the creature hit. It snapped at her, its breath foul in her face. From her left she could hear a yelp. *Alyssa!* But she had to deal with this dog first. Holding the dog's throat with her left hand, she swung with all her strength for the dog's ribs with her right. The knife plunged into the dog, and she could feel the blade scrape a rib as the knife went in up to the hilt. She pulled it out as she rolled over, the dog thrashing, and once on top, she stabbed it again. The dog screamed and she rolled to her feet in a crouch. *Where's Alyssa?*

In front of her, Alyssa stood over the first dog, Kyra's knife in her hand, blood dripping from the tip. The dog lay at her feet, unmoving. Kyra ran to her. "Are you all right?"

Alyssa stared at the dog, her eyes filling with tears. "I had to, Kyra. It was getting up. Getting ready to kill you."

Kyra reached out and took the knife. "You had to do it, Alyssa."

She sank to her knees and stroked the dog's fur. "They were just hungry, Kyra."

"Maybe so, Alyssa. But that doesn't mean we had to be their meal."

"I'm supposed to be a healer, not a killer."

"You aren't a killer, Alyssa. You protected yourself and me. Thank you. But that doesn't make you a killer."

Kyra pulled her friend up by her hand and walked her to the fire. She pulled some wood sorrel out of a pocket and dropped it in the pot of water and set it next to the fire. "Some tea will help. Take it off just before it boils, okay?"

Alyssa blinked at her. "What will you be doing?"

"I'm going to drag these dogs away from the camp and skin them. We'll need the furs in the winter. "

Alyssa paled. "Do you have to?" Her voice quavered.

"If I don't, they'll be wasted. Why shouldn't we take the furs? We'll need them this winter. The bodies will be left for the scavengers."

Kyra could see her sigh and watched a tear roll down one cheek, glistening in the firelight.

"Yes. I suppose so."

"You'll have to heal the toxins from them, then from me, before I start."

Alyssa nodded, shoulders slumped. She rose and walked hesitantly to the dog she'd killed. Kneeling, she ran her hands over the animal's fur. It was a gentle movement, petting the dog, almost an apology. When she finished with all three she went back to the fire and stroked Kyra's whole body. "I'm sorry," she whispered when Kyra tensed. "I know how private you are but I have to be sure there're no toxins on you."

Kyra unclenched her teeth when Alyssa finished. "S'all right. Has to be done. I'll get to work."

It took two hours and when she came back into camp she was bloody but had three skins rolled tightly. She used water from her bottle to rinse off and wash her hands and face. She left the skins away from the tent. When she finally sank down in front of the fire, Alyssa handed her a cup of tea. "I'm sorry I couldn't help you."

Kyra held the cup under her nose. The lemony scent of the wood sorrel helped clear her nose of the smell of blood and death. "That's all right." She drank the hot tea down. It tasted heavenly. "It's done now. I'll make dinner in just a minute."

Alyssa handed her the pot. "I made dinner. It seemed the least I could do after you protected me."

Kyra blinked. Alyssa hadn't done any camp work except to clean the water since they started. She took the pot; it held macaroni and cheese.

"I figured you could use your favorite."

"Thank you, Alyssa. That was thoughtful." She realized she was starving so she dug in. No meal had ever tasted so good.

As she scraped the last bits from the pot, Alyssa said, "I think it's time I did my share of the camp work."

Kyra stopped with the spoon halfway to her mouth. "Sure, if you're not too tired from healing. I'd like that."

Alyssa made more tea in Kyra's enamel cup and passed it across the fire. She took the pot and spoon and scrubbed them out with grass. "Good." She smiled at her friend across the flames.

THEY ARRIVE AT THEIR FIRST SURVIVOR
COMMUNITY

When they started out the next morning, Alyssa was even more quiet than usual. At their morning break, Kyra broke the silence. "What's the matter?"

Alyssa was leaning against her pack, back against the tree with her eyes closed. "I don't think I'm cut out for the dangerous stuff." Her green eyes opened to gaze at her friend. "I wasn't much help yesterday."

Kyra snorted. "You had my back when I was wrestling with that damn dog. I think you have what it takes."

Alyssa sat forward. "How do you know how to fight like that?"

Kyra sipped from her bottle, then recapped it immediately. She'd knocked an open bottle of water over the second day out from the school. It had been hours before they came to another stream to replenish her supply. Now she recapped or recovered everything, as soon as it left her mouth. "You know Malcolm taught all of us how to use weapons, self-defense, all that stuff."

Alyssa smiled. "I wasn't interested in that, but yes; I could have joined the other kids if I had wanted to."

"Well, when I told Malcolm what we planned to do, he gave me extra lessons. He taught me how to fight someone bigger than I am, how to fight more than one person, how to fight animals. I carried massive bruises for months."

"He saved our lives, then." Alyssa chewed her lower lip, her delicate face a study in anxiety. "I can feel them, you know."

It was Kyra's turn to sit forward. "What do you mean?"

"It's how I can heal. I can feel the living plant, identify what's wrong and make it right." She looked at the ground and picked up a brown pine needle, twisting it between thumb and forefinger. "I could feel the dog's life and I snuffed it out." Tears flowed down her cheeks, falling silently to the ground.

Kyra crawled the three feet to her friend. She put her arm around Alyssa's shoulders. "That's tough, as sensitive as you are to the life around you. That makes you all the more brave for it."

The slender girl sniffled and wiped her eyes with the heel of her hand. "I suppose. I couldn't let the animal kill us."

Kyra squeezed her again. "That's right. We have a right to live, too."

The women moved on and for the next two weeks they worked on finding the right rhythm for themselves. Kyra still did most of the camp work in the evening; Alyssa was drained from healing their way across the countryside. But in the mornings, she was the one who made tea and breakfast and cleaned the dishes while Kyra took down the tent. The first time it rained, Kyra panicked until Alyssa declared the rain clean. They stripped and bathed in the shower, rinsing their clothing of sweat and dirt in the rain, then wrapped themselves in their sleeping bags. The patter of rain on the tent made them sleepy, so they rested the remainder of the day.

They were four weeks away from their school when they crested a hill and saw a town in front of them. "You think there are any survivors here?" Alyssa asked.

"Hard to tell; there weren't any in the last few towns. We'll check the schools, and any other big buildings where people could have sheltered."

"Wait." Alyssa pointed to the east side of the town. "Is that smoke?"

Kyra squinted in the mid-morning light. "Yeah. That's smoke coming from what looks like a factory. They must have some sort of water inside the building, like we did."

"New people, Kyra. Won't that be interesting?" Her green eyes sparkled with excitement.

Kyra thought about Malcolm's warnings concerning other survivors. "It's a vicious world, kiddo," he'd told her. "If you find any survivors, they're going to be tough and mean. Anything or anyone new is more than likely going to be viewed as a threat."

"That seems kind of negative, Malcolm. We're not mean," she remembered saying.

"Maybe, maybe not," he'd said. "But if someone came knocking on our front door I'd be very suspicious."

She pulled her thoughts back to Alyssa's question. "They may be interesting. They may look at us like those dogs did, another meal to be had. We'll have to see." She turned to Alyssa. "Don't offer any information about where the school is or the town we're from, at least not at first."

Alyssa's eyebrows went up. "Why not?"

"Because we've left a trail back to them. If these are good people, that won't be a problem. If they aren't, well, no sense handing out directions."

"Ah." Alyssa nodded. "I'm going to have to tell them about what I can do. How else can we explain how we got here?"

Kyra scratched her neck where her braid lay. Little hairs were coming loose and making her itch. "I've been thinking about that for over a year. I talked to Malcolm about it, too. There's no good answer. I'd like to avoid talking about it at first, if we can. Who knows how people will react when they find out you have "magic" power?"

"It's not magic, Kyra."

"I know that, but they may not believe it. So let's take it slow, okay?"

Alyssa adjusted her pack. "Yeah. Makes sense. Shall we go?"

"Sure," Kyra hitched her pack up. "Down the hill and to the east. Let's hope we can get a look at the place before we knock on the front door."

\#

Kyra banged on the door of the factory with her bow. It had taken all day to get here and the sun was setting. Her stomach was in a knot as she waited for an answer, Alyssa standing behind her. They'd washed her hands after she healed a path up to and including the door. Kyra hoped they would be nice people, glad to have news that there were other survivors, but Malcolm's warnings weren't encouraging. She rapped the bow on the door again; the metal door had a hollow echo.

It took a few minutes before they saw an eye peeking around the edge of the window. They could hear people inside, barely contained panic in their voices. Soon there was the sound of metal scraping across cement and of chains being removed from the doors.

Kyra and Alyssa exchanged glances. Their refuge had never been locked, chained or barred. There was no need. Who was around to come inside after the rain first started? The door had to be forced open; it seemed to have rusted in place. After a screech that echoed down the street, a male face peered out of the five-inch crack. "Who are you?"

The women had agreed that Kyra would be the speaker. She told the pale, dark haired visage, "I'm Kyra, this is my friend Alyssa. We're traveling and saw the smoke from your chimney. We thought you'd like to know that there are other survivors."

The man ducked back around the door. The women could hear urgent whispering just inside. The head popped back around the door. "I'm Dan. This is the Community of the Children of God, Survivors of the Cursed Rain." He stared at them.

Kyra wondered what he was waiting for. "We're happy to meet you, Dan."

A whisper was heard from inside, and Dan nodded. "We need to move the door so you can come inside, if you'd like?"

"Yes." Kyra put on a smile even though she wasn't getting a good feeling about this. "We'd love to share stories with you."

Dan disappeared again and soon several sets of men's hands were pulling the door open. When the screeching of steel against concrete stopped and the dust had settled, Dan reappeared. "Please come in and meet the community."

Kyra felt as though it was some sort of trap but she'd already told them they would visit. She sighed, pasted on her smile and stepped inside the door, Alyssa behind her. Once inside, Kyra saw they were in a hallway in what looked like the office spaces of the factory. The walls were a dingy green though the space was well lit by daylight filtering through the dirty windows and the open door. The hallway was lined with several men who all stared at Kyra and Alyssa.

Kyra felt her hands begin to sweat. "I'm so happy that we've found survivors."

Dan nodded. "We are blessed indeed that you have come. Follow me. It's time to eat."

The two followed Dan through a labyrinth of hallways and open spaces until they reached a large space with tables set up in a communal dining room. This was comforting to Kyra, as their own community ate communally in the school cafeteria. What was uncomfortable were all of the eyes staring at them. Kyra had begun to think there were only men here until they reached the dining area. There she saw women setting the tables and bringing food out from the cooking area. Children ran around the space, playing tag until they saw the newcomers. They stopped to stare, too. Kyra's mouth went dry. She could feel Alyssa very close to her back.

Dan showed them to a table and invited them to sit. He sat down with them after they dropped their packs on the floor behind their chairs. They were joined by a teenaged boy, a girl who looked to be a little younger than him, and two smaller boys. They stared at the visitors. A woman hurried over and poured water into the glasses in front of each plate. She eyed the pelts attached to Kyra's pack and sniffed at the reek. Kyra expected an introduction but the woman hurried off. She came back moments later with a pot of stew and placed it on the table, then sat in the chair next to Dan.

At the front of the room, a man stood up. "Let us pray." Kyra noticed that even the children looked down and raised their hands to the ceiling. The room went silent immediately and he intoned, "Dear Lord our God in Heaven. Bless us this day for our daily bread. Forgive us our sins as you forgave those of your dear son, Jesus. Thank you, Lord, for the gift of visitors to our community. We ask that you protect us and guide us, today and every day. In Our Father's name, Amen."

"Amen," the community at the tables repeated.

Dan took his hands down and the rest of the table followed. "Welcome, Kyra and Alyssa. This is my wife, Ruth, my son," he pointed to the teen boy, "Andrew, my sons, Garth and Howard, and my daughter, Jessica."

Kyra looked at the wife first. "Nice to meet you, Ruth. I'm Kyra and this is my friend, Alyssa." She turned to the children. "Nice to meet all of you." The little boys stared, the teen boy sat up straighter but the wife and the teen girl both refused to look Kyra in the eyes. Ruth stood up and, serving the visitors first, scooped stew into the bowls. Her husband was next, then the boys, oldest to youngest. The girl was served, then Ruth scraped what was left in the pot into her bowl. There was only about half of what everyone else had. She sat down in her chair, put her hands in her lap, and stared at her food.

Dan picked up his spoon and began to eat. The boys did too, then the girl, then Ruth. Kyra and Alyssa exchanged a quick glance, then began their meal.

"Thank you so much for sharing your food. That's very generous of you," Kyra said as she spooned up a bit of the stew. She blew on it, then tasted. Like in her community, the stew was vegetarian. It's seasoned well so they must have salt, she thought. "It's very good, Ruth," she said after she finished the first spoonful.

Ruth's spoon stopped halfway to her mouth, she stared a moment, then her eyes, both surprised and frightened, went back to her plate. Dan glared at Ruth, then returned his gaze to the visitors. "It's our custom that women not speak at the table."

Kyra blinked, her mouth full of stew. She quickly swallowed. "You don't talk at meals?"

The boys fidgeted in their seats and stared at Kyra.

"No, men talk. Women listen."

She bent her head in acknowledgement and shot a quick glance at Alyssa. She gave a barely perceptible shrug and dipped up another spoonful of stew. Kyra's mind was racing. *What kind of place is this? Ruth looks terrified.*

She gazed around the dining area. At each table, only the men were talking. Women and children were silent, eyes on their food. The meal went quickly as each person focused on eating. As soon as Dan was finished, Ruth leapt up and took his bowl and spoon. She gathered hers up and then the girl's bowl, the small boy's and the teen boy's and then Kyra's and Alyssa's. Kyra had just finished eating but Alyssa still had half a bowl of food. She noticed the children had eaten all of theirs.

"Come," said Dan. "I'll show you the facilities and then your room. You must be tired."

The two stood up, picked up their packs and followed Dan. He showed them the restrooms, modified from the original factory arrangement so that the waste went outside the wall. "Rinse your deposit out of the tube with the water in the bucket," he told them. Nearby he showed them the shower area, also divided into a men's and women's side. "We heat the water with sunlight," he explained proudly. "Hot showers."

Kyra had to admit a hot shower sounded nice. Her community,

while it had running water from the spring the Catholic School was famous for, had only cold showers. They'd never heated it. After the shower room he took them along a makeshift hallway. It was obvious this was built after the people took shelter in the factory. Kyra was surprised to find that he showed them into a real room. "We've put beds in here and the door locks." He looked a little nervous. "For your privacy."

"Thank you, Dan," Kyra said as she looked around the room. Lit by a single smoky lamp burning what smelled like fuel oil, it seemed to have been a storage room. The ten-by-fifteen foot space was windowless. The walls were peeling industrial green paint while the floor was bare cement. Two beds were against the facing side walls. "We'll be very comfortable here."

"In the morning after breakfast, our leader Joseph will meet with you. He'll explain everything." Dan stared at the two young women. Kyra felt as though he were eyeing a piece of meat.

"We look forward to meeting him, Dan. Thank you for your help today." Kyra remained in the middle of the room and waited, Alyssa behind her.

Dan nodded and backed out of the door. "Um, unless you're visiting the facilities, it's best you stay in here. The old equipment in the factory can be dangerous."

"Good advice, Dan," Kyra said as she pasted on a smile. "Thanks for the word of caution."

"Good night," he said and closed the door.

Kyra breathed a sigh of relief, pulled her pack off and dropped it on the right-hand bed. Alyssa stared at the door. "Does this feel wrong to you?" she asked.

"It does." Kyra tried the bed. It wasn't too bad, better than sleeping on the ground. "We'll go to the bathroom, wash up, then get back in here. No one goes without the other one, okay?"

Alyssa pulled her pack off and set it on the floor beside her bed. "Agreed. This place is creeping me out."

Kyra nodded. "Me, too."

ALYSSA AND KYRA MEET THE LEADER

Oatmeal was the meal in the morning. Again, everyone ate in family groups and again hands were raised in prayer. Dan glared at Kyra and Alyssa when they kept their hands in their laps but Kyra didn't care. She didn't belong to this religion and she wasn't going to pretend. Having gone to bed hungry, Alyssa gobbled her breakfast, causing her to hiccup. The boys at the end of the table started to giggle. One look from their father silenced them and earned the two young women another glare.

Kyra noticed that Ruth winced as she was seated and when she rose to gather the bowls. She was about to ask if the woman was all right when Dan said, "I'm to take you to our leader, Joseph, this morning. Prepare yourselves. I'll collect you from your room when he's ready."

Alyssa started to protest but Kyra put a hand on her thigh. Alyssa glared at Kyra but Kyra gave a minute shake of her head.

She smiled. "Certainly, Dan. We're looking forward to meeting him."

In their room, Alyssa rounded on her friend. "What are you doing, Kyra? I'm here to heal, not sit around inside." Her green eyes flashed with anger. "There's work to be done."

Kyra held up her hand. "I understand. But I want to take this slow. No one has asked us any questions. Not 'where are you from?' Not 'how did you get here?' And last night after supper we discussed the way women and children are treated. We need to see this leader. Find out what's going on, then make decisions about staying or going."

"Maybe," Alyssa huffed. She flung her fine, nearly white hair over her shoulder. "I suppose I can go through my things and do repairs and cleaning while we wait."

"That's the spirit." Kyra grinned. "It's nice to have the time and space to spread things out and see what we need to fix."

The two worked quietly on their gear for two hours. Everything was hung to dry. Even with the toxic rain, the woods were constantly damp. They made a trip to the bathroom together. Back in the room, Kyra took off her hiking boots and stretched out on the bed while Alyssa paced back and forth in the room, her fine hair flying out behind her. "What's taking so long?"

"Hard telling. I imagine that the leader has a lot going on, just as Malcolm did."

Alyssa nodded. "I suppose." She flopped down on her bed. "You know, it looks as though they cleared this room just for us." She pointed at the floor. "There are rust stains on the floor where steel cabinets used to be."

Kyra grunted, her hands behind her head and her eyes closed as she lay on her bed. "I noticed that last night. I'm pretty sure most people are housed in makeshift rooms in one of the warehouse spaces. To give us a lockable room seems either very generous or a way to keep us separate from the rest of the community."

"I think--" Alyssa began to say when there was a knock at the door. Her head whipped around at the noise. Kyra leaned up on her elbows, her feet still crossed over each other.

"Come in."

Dan opened the door. "Joseph is ready to see you now."

Kyra smiled at the man. "Thank you, Dan." She swung her feet over the side of the bed and put on her boots. "I just have to tie my shoes and I'm ready."

Alyssa stood up while Dan watched Kyra tie her shoes. "You brought two men with you, Dan?" she asked when she glanced out the door.

He struggled to control his face but Kyra could tell he was experiencing conflicting emotions. *Was that shame that he'd been called on it, or fear, or shock?* She couldn't tell. "I'm ready now." She stood up. "Lead on, Dan."

The eyebrows of the two men in the hallway twitched and a flash of shock spread across their faces, then they recovered and stared at the two women blank-faced. She realized they were the same size as Malcolm and looked quite strong. When Kyra reached the door, they marched ahead of the two women with Dan trailing behind. Kyra heard him shut and lock the door. She chewed her lip but kept her face pleasant for the men that lined the hallway. She kept track of the windows they passed, estimating where the sun was and what direction they went.

They found themselves in a short hallway with two office doors on each side of the hall and a door at the end. One of the men ahead of her--she'd started thinking of them as guards--rapped on the door and opened it. Kyra and Alyssa entered a room more finely decorated than any they'd ever seen.

In front of them was a wooden desk, gleaming with polish. Oriental carpets were on the floor and drapes of some shiny embossed gold material hung from the windows. Kyra noted that the windows to the desk's right had the morning sun coming through them, the light shining across the desk. The window behind the desk looked out to the front of the building. Instead of the industrial green of the hall walls, this room had been painted white. Fine furniture was placed around the room and vases and religious icons decorated the tables. The room had to be twenty by thirty feet.

The two guards moved to either side of the door and stood, hands clasped in front of them. Dan followed them in and moved to stand just in front of them at the desk. "Joseph, this is Kyra and Alyssa, our visitors." He nervously stroked his beard, which reached his chest, then stepped to his left to stand at the end of the desk

Kyra and Alyssa stepped forward. There were no chairs there. Joseph looked up from a Bible; bright blue eyes stared at them. He closed the book softly, then stood up. "Ladies." He reached across the desk in an offer of a handshake. "Welcome to the Community of the Children of God."

Kyra stepped forward and shook with him. She was surprised at the strength in the hand. Then Alyssa did so. She massaged her hand when she got it back, her eyebrows furrowed.

"Thank you for allowing us inside your community, Joseph," Kyra began. Dan, to Kyra's left, raised his hand, it looked as though he was going to correct her, but Joseph waved him off. It was a small movement at his waist but Dan stopped dead in his tracks and moved to stand behind and to the right his leader's chair. Joseph sat down.

"I have to say I was surprised when you knocked on our door yesterday." He adjusted the fall of his beard. It had grown to the man's waist. He stroked it smooth. "I told Dan to make you comfortable and refrain from questions. I know you must have been tired from your journey."

"We appreciate that, Joseph. It has been a hard journey," Kyra responded.

"The Lord gives us strength to follow his path," he intoned.

His thin face and sunken cheeks gave him a skeletal look. Kyra was made a little uncomfortable by the man's appearance and demeanor. She didn't know what to say to such a meaningless phrase. "Uh, thank you."

"Where are you from?" Joseph asked. He folded his hands on the desk, eyes focused on hers.

"Our community is many days away," Kyra said, put off by the direct stare. "The trip was dangerous. We were attacked by feral dogs."

"The good Lord has saved you to reach us," he said in a solemn baritone. "God was looking out for you."

Kyra knitted her brows together. *What is wrong with this man? He's worse than the nuns.* "I suppose so. We began our journey a little over a month ago. We always wanted to know if there were any other survivors."

"And where you came from, they were godless?" Joseph asked. He sat forward, eager to hear the answer.

Kyra shot a glance at Alyssa, who shrugged.

"No, in our town the Catholic church and school were the civil defense shelter. The original Catholic mission was founded there because of a spring. It never fails and provided us with clean water. All the rest came from the civil defense supplies, long gone now. The nuns took in refugees from the rain and nearly died themselves trying to save everyone who came."

"Papists," Joseph spat. Behind him, Dan wrinkled his nose in disgust. "It's no wonder then that you two escaped."

Kyra shook her head slowly from side to side. "No, we didn't escape. They sent us off with as many necessary supplies as they could spare."

He settled back into his chair. "And you have rubber suits? That's what our men need to gather supplies from the town."

"No. My friend, Alyssa, can heal the plants that suffer under the remains of the brown rain. She healed us a path. We want to do for you what we did for our community: clear land for you to grow crops, to get outside and enjoy the sun, the outdoors."

She turned at the sound of gasps behind her. The two guards stared wide-eyed. When she turned back, Dan was whispering in Joseph's ear. Alyssa sidled closer to her friend.

"Interesting concept," Joseph said. "Can you show me?" He stood up.

Kyra cocked an eyebrow. She didn't expect such sudden acceptance. "Sure. We need to go outside."

Joseph nodded. The guards opened the door and Joseph strode forward. Kyra and Alyssa followed and Dan came behind, with the guards bringing up the rear. The leader walked briskly along the hallways. They turned left outside the office area and through the middle of the makeshift halls. Women and children scattered in front of him, eyes focused on the floor. After several turns, Joseph came to a large warehouse door. He flicked his hand and the two bodyguards, three-inch beards quivering, opened the huge door with ropes. The door screeched but not as much as the front door had.

They must open this door once in awhile, Kyra thought as Alyssa held her hand. Dan glared at them and Alyssa dropped it. Ah, she thought as the door slowly crept up. *This opens to the west.* Three rusted semis and their trailers sat in the parking lot. Past that, there was a dreary field where hardly any green showed. The guards tied off the door pulls and stood beside the open door. Joseph waved the two women forward to stand beside him on the edge. The sun was just beginning to come around the building and shine into the door.

"We open this, occasionally," he told them as he crossed his hands in front of him. Dan stood half a step behind and to Joseph's right.

Outside the door Kyra could see where part of the cement loading dock had been scraped clean of the brown rain, especially in front of the door.

"Can you clean this space?" he asked Alyssa.

"I do better at healing plants." She looked from the dock to his face. "But yes, I can clean it, just as I cleaned your front door so we could knock on it."

He waved his right hand in an invitation to go ahead.

Alyssa looked to Kyra. "Go ahead, Alyssa. It needs to be cleaned so they can get down and across the parking lot to the land."

The young woman nodded and took a deep breath as she gazed out over the dock. She stepped forward and bent down, her hands passing along the cement. While Joseph, Dan, and the bodyguards watched, the rest of the community crept forward to see what was going on.

A large woman who looked better fed than any of the other women that Kyra had seen, marched up and stood half a step behind and to the left of Joseph. "Husband."

He turned slightly toward her. "Wife. Meet Kyra." He nodded at her. "And Alyssa." He nodded toward the loading dock. "She claims she can clean the brown sludge away."

The woman's round face stared at Alyssa. After a moment she turned to Kyra. Hard, gray eyes bored into the young woman. "Are you saved, child?"

Kyra blinked. Alyssa was out there, cleaning a way for them to get out of this factory and this is what the woman asks? "I didn't get your name."

The woman went red to the roots of the gray hair tied up into a severe bun at the back of her head. "I'm Glenna, wife of Joseph. Are you saved?"

"I was baptized by the nuns in our community," Kyra said. The men were so disdainful of the Catholics; she wondered how this woman would react.

Her eyes opened wide. "Not sufficient. We'll take care of that."

Not if I can help it, Kyra thought.

Glenna peered at Kyra. "You are unmarried?"

Kyra nodded. "I take care of Alyssa."

Glenna frowned, leaned over and whispered to her husband. He never took his eyes off of Alyssa, but nodded in response.

Glenna stopped asking questions. She ordered a chair for her husband and a boy, about twelve, came running up a few minutes later to place the chair behind Joseph. The leader sat without looking. The boy drifted back into the crowd.

Alyssa worked for two hours and, by the end, had cleaned the whole dock, the steps down to the parking lot and a short path across it. She climbed back up the stairs and stood at the door. "Before I come in, I need clean water to wash my hands."

Glenna snapped her fingers. A young woman holding a tray with a pitcher of water and a glass came forward. Glenna handed Kyra the pitcher. The friends stepped over to the edge of the dock and Kyra poured the water over Alyssa's hands. Clean, they came back to the door. Joseph stood up.

"Interesting." He turned and walked away, his community parting before him.

Dan signaled the guards and they lowered the door. "I'll take you back to your room."

COMMANDED TO DO CHORES

Kyra wasn't happy. It was only mid-day and she didn't want to spend the rest of the day in a dark room. "Dan, it's too early for bed. We'd prefer to stay out here, with the rest of the community." The nearby women and children stared. The guard's eyes went wide. Dan, standing next to Kyra, raised his hand. Kyra stepped back and into a defensive pose. She could hear a gasp from the women but she wasn't going to get slapped by this man. He turned red and dropped his hand.

Alyssa had slipped behind her. Dan glared first at Kyra then at the remaining women and children. Kyra, still in her pose, could hear women shushing the children and the faint shuffle of bare feet moving away. She never took her eyes off of Dan. The two guards stepped forward, one on each side of him. He held up his hand in a signal to stop.

"I'm afraid," he struggled to get his voice under control. "I'm afraid you've made a serious breach in etiquette."

"How so?" Kyra asked, her gray-blue eyes focused on his brown ones. If he made a move, she was close enough to kick him in the head. She could see his mouth work.

"Women do as they're told. Women do not question any man, especially the second-in-command of this community."

"We are visitors here. Where we are from men do not hit women or children." She glanced at the guards; their mouths hung open. She brought her eyes back to Dan. He was clenching his fists. "However, we're guests here." Kyra came out of her defensive pose. "It seems only fair that we do our fair share. Many hands make light work, the nuns used to tell us. Alyssa is very good with growing things. She can help with your garden. I do most anything; equipment repair, cleaning, laundry, dishes, it doesn't matter to me."

One of the guards took half a step forward and whispered to Dan. Dan took a deep breath and unclenched his fists, wiping them on his trousers. "Yes, that seems fair." He waved at the guard who whispered to him. "Take Alyssa to the grow room." The guard nodded and motioned to Alyssa to follow him.

"Kyra," Alyssa said softly.

"Go ahead, Alyssa. We'll meet at supper time." The last was said as she gave Dan a piercing look.

"Yes. You'll meet at supper. My family's table."

Kyra nodded and Alyssa followed the guard.

"Henry, take Kyra to the kitchens. Put her to work with Barbara."

Stone-faced, the guard waved to Kyra. She nodded to Dan. "Thank you, Dan." He grunted as she followed the guard.

In the kitchen the guard stopped behind a girl of about fifteen though to Kyra it was hard to tell. The girl was thin to the point of emaciation and short, at least a hand shorter than Kyra. ⌐ girl was bent over a huge pot, scrubbing.

"Barbara," the guard shouted.

The girl sprang straight up, hazel eyes wide. Her brown hair was matted and she was obviously afraid.

"This person, Kyra, will work with you this afternoon." He sniffed and turned away. Women and children all over the kitchen stared.

Kyra stepped forward and held out her hand. "Hi, I'm Kyra and I'm new here."

The girl backed up a step, staring at Kyra's hand as though it would bite. Her eyes flashed to the rest of the women in the room. Dan's wife, Ruth, clapped her hands. "Back to work." The others drifted back to their jobs, sneaking occasional glances at the newcomer.

"Let me help you," Kyra said.

Again, Barbara's eyes went to Ruth.

"You heard the man," Ruth snapped. "He said she's to help you. Get on with it."

Barbara ducked her head in acknowledgement and handed Kyra a worn pumice stone. "Clean the pot. Nothing is to be left inside. We get beat if there's any food left inside."

Kyra arched an eyebrow and took the stone. "I'll do a good job, Barbara."

The girl ran off and Kyra shrugged. She bent over the pot and began to scrub at the cooked-on mess on the sides. In a moment, Barbara returned with another stone and started scrubbing on the other side. It wasn't until they finished scrubbing and Barbara brought water to rinse the pot that she whispered a question. "You really from another community?"

"Mmhmm," Kyra voiced. "A long way from here."

Barbara looked around the kitchen out of the corner of her eyes. "Why'd you come here?"

They sopped up the first rinse of the pot with rags, then rinsed again. "Well, Alyssa and I are exploring. We wanted to know if there were any other survivors."

"You don't want to be here," the girl whispered.

"Barbara!" Ruth shouted. "Less talking more working."

"Yes, ma'am," the girl's voice echoed up out of the pot.

"Finish that up and get on to scrubbing the dining room floor." Ruth looked at Kyra and fidgeted with the collar of her dress. Kyra realized the woman was unsure if she should order her out there or not.

"All clean here, Ruth." Kyra stood up and dropped her rag in Barbara's bowl. "We'll get right on the floor."

Barbara and Ruth both stared at her.

"Where do you keep the floor cleaning supplies, Barbara?"

#

Alyssa and Kyra met just before dinner. "How'd it go?" Kyra asked Alyssa over the noise of kids running through the dining area.

"Their garden is dying," Alyssa whispered back. "I spent the entire afternoon saving their plants. I'm exhausted. How about you?"

Kyra held out her hands. They were red and swollen. "All afternoon scrubbing this floor on my hands and knees with a teen girl named Barbara. You should see…"

Dan walked up to them. "Kyra, Alyssa. Let us break our fast."

Kyra smiled. "Certainly, Dan."

Dinner was a repeat of the night before. Afterward, again, Dan escorted them to their room, lit the lamp and left them there for the night.

"What were you saying earlier?" Alyssa asked as she sank down on her bed.

"Oh, the girl, Barbara. She doesn't have any family, so she has no male protector. She's the bottom of the entire community totem pole. All of the worst scut work goes to her, all of the time. There's no rotation like at home. I didn't ask but from the look of her, she gets the least to eat of anyone here."

"Oh, poor thing." Alyssa's face wrinkled in a show of distress. "How awful."

"Did you make any friends today?" Kyra took off her boots and set them just under the edge of her bed. She wanted to be able to find them in the dark.

"No, but the head gardener hovered over me all day. Once in a while he'd ask questions but mainly I think he was there to make sure I didn't talk to anyone else."

Kyra nodded and lay back on the bed. "Yeah, every time Ruth caught me or Barbara talking, she yelled at Barbara. I stopped after a while. I didn't want to get her in trouble."

Alyssa rubbed her face, her green eyes troubled. "This is an unhappy place."

"That's for sure," Kyra said.

The next morning at breakfast, Ruth stood up and looked at the visitors and her daughter, Jessica. "Girls, you will gather the dishes and bring them to the kitchen today."

Alyssa and Kyra exchanged glances. Kyra shrugged and picked up her bowl and spoon. Alyssa followed. Jessica grabbed her brother's bowls while Kyra picked up Ruth's and Dan's. The three young women followed Ruth into the kitchen.

They put the bowls and spoons down at an industrial sink where everyone else was putting theirs, then they turned to leave. "You can't go." Ruth's mouth drew into a thin line, her hands clasped in a knot in front of her. "Kyra is to work here and Alyssa is to go back to the gardens."

The pair turned to stare at Ruth. "I don't think so," Kyra said.

"No," Alyssa said at the same time. "I'm going out to heal the grounds so you can plant outside."

"No." Ruth closed in on them. Kyra could see her wince and put a hand to her left ribs. "You have orders to go to your assigned jobs."

Kyra folded her arms. "We said no. We aren't here to work in the kitchen. Alyssa is going outside to heal the earth and I'm going with her to protect her."

The two turned and walked off. In their room they each put the strap of their water bottles, filled that morning before breakfast, over their heads. Kyra grabbed her bow and quiver and they headed for the warehouse door. Kyra snagged a teenage boy and made him pull on the second rope. When he tied his off, he ran.

"He's going straight to Dan or Joseph," Alyssa said as they watched him race away.

"Phhttt," Kyra blew air between her lips. "I don't care, do you?"

Alyssa shrugged. "Let's get to work."

They walked out onto the dock, down the steps and to the end of the four-foot-wide path that Alyssa had started yesterday. "It's about two hundred feet to the grass, Alyssa."

"No problem." She began to work.

The two had gone about twenty feet when Glenna appeared in the warehouse door. She didn't step foot out onto the dock. "You come in here right now!" she yelled.

Kyra turned to look. Behind Glenna, Ruth and several other women crowded the doorway. "I don't think so. We're doing the work we're supposed to be doing."

"You'll be sorry, young woman." She turned and huffed back inside, the rest following her.

When Kyra turned to look again, the two guards from yesterday stood in the door, arms folded across their chests, glaring. Kyra grinned and waved, then went back to watching the wood line. By the time Jessica came to the doorway and called them to dinner, Alyssa had cleared a wide path to the grass and nearly an acre of lawn and into the woods. Kyra poured the remainder of her water over Alyssa's hands and the two went back to the door. The guards had untied the ropes and had the door half closed when they scooted inside.

They went to the washroom to clean up, then Kyra put her bow and quiver and their refilled water bottles in their room. When they got to the dining room, everyone was seated. Dan glared. He rose and raised his hands and gave the grace. Again, neither Kyra nor Alyssa participated. Ruth came to the table and put a bowl down in front of each young woman. Kyra looked up at her. "What's this?" She could see everyone else had vegetable stew in front of them.

Their bowls had broth.

Ruth sat down and focused on her bowl. Dan spoke. "This is what troublemakers get for anti-social behavior."

Kyra could feel her face flush. "Alyssa has expended a great deal of energy. She needs food."

He shrugged and picked up his spoon, slowly and deliberately scooping a large bite. "Maybe tomorrow you'll remember that."

They were halfway through the thin broth when Joseph walked into the room. Everyone rose but Kyra and Alyssa. He waved them back to their seats. "I think today is a good day for a story," he began in that rich baritone that reached every corner of the room. "This is a tale of the grasshopper and the ant. A long time ago, before the Lord smote this Earth and rid it of all of the blasphemers, adulterers and sinners, the ant worked very hard. The ant lived in a community, much like this." He waved his hand around the room to indicate all of them. "Each ant knew its place in the order of the community and they worked hard, everyone doing his or her duty." He glanced at the two visitors.

"Then one day a grasshopper appeared at their door. 'Help me,' the grasshopper said. 'It's a cruel world and I'm starving.' Well," he looked at individual people in the crowd. She followed his gaze and noticed Barbara, seated on a stool near the kitchen door, a bowl in her lap, already scraped clean. "The ants fed the grasshopper and in return, asked the grasshopper if he would help them with the work of the community."

He waved his arms wide. "Of course!" the grasshopper said. "I'd be happy to help. And so the grasshopper did, for awhile. The next thing the ants knew, the grasshopper was outside, enjoying the fresh air and didn't return until dinnertime that night."

Joseph turned, walked over to Kyra and Alyssa and stood behind their seats. "He sat down with the ants, who had worked hard all day and expected to be fed."

"What do you think the ants did?" he asked the crowd.

A male voice in the back shouted, "They didn't feed the grasshopper."

Joseph grinned, a cadaverous grin with yellow teeth. Kyra began to blush from both shame and anger. "Pretty close, Brother, pretty close. It wouldn't be Christian to starve the creature, so the ants gave the grasshopper a little to eat in hopes that on the morrow he'd take more care to pitch in."

Kyra's hands turned to fists in her lap. It was an effort of will to keep her head up and her eyes forward. She glared at Dan, who smirked back at her.

"The moral of the tale?" Joseph asked. "We'll have to see, won't we?" He nodded to Dan, then turned and strode out of the dining room.

Kyra picked up her bowl and drank the broth. She elbowed Alyssa, and she did the same. Since Dan was done, she picked up his bowl and spoon and Ruth's and walked straight back into the kitchen, Alyssa behind her with her own bowl and spoon. They went directly to their room and shut the door.

DEFIANCE

The next morning, breakfast for the two friends was oatmeal watered down until there was nearly no cereal in it. Alyssa and Kyra drank it down and rose, without apology and before Dan finished. They had brought their water, the bow and quiver, and a bit of dried food Kyra had stashed as emergency rations. Kyra already had a headache and on the way to the warehouse door her stomach growled so loud that Alyssa turned her head to stare. They began to laugh.

"Well, I feel the same way," Alyssa told her friend. "Maybe when they see what we're doing, they'll be more understanding.

Kyra grunted.

When they reached the door, the two guards were there. "Joseph does not want you outside," the big man called Henry said. "It's dangerous and the brown sludge is poisonous."

"Not to me," Alyssa said. She stood tall and stared the men down. "Are you going to open that door or do we need to do it."

Henry shrugged and signaled to his partner. They stepped to the ropes and pulled. Kyra and Alyssa didn't wait for them to tie the ropes off; they ducked under the door as soon as it was high enough. By the time the door was fully open, the two were out at the edge of the cleared space.

Alyssa followed a bit of lawn around the edge of the wood and began to clear another area, an abandoned field. By mid-morning she'd cleared the whole plot and some more of the nearby woods.

"Why the woods, Alyssa?" Kyra asked. She'd been keeping an eye on the guards still standing in the warehouse door. They never stepped out on the dock.

Alyssa stood up and stretched. "These are nut trees." She pointed to a stand of trees that looked much like every other tree to Kyra. "I did the same back home. They'll be able to gather the nuts and add a good source of protein to their diets. They'll attract animals too, squirrels, deer, who knows. But the people here may someday choose to hunt again and the meat will be a welcome addition to their diets."

Kyra sniffed. "Being pretty generous to people who haven't fed us in a day and a half."

"Not much I can do about that. Their road is their own. I will continue to help as long as I have the strength."

Alyssa went back to healing and after scanning the wood's edge, Kyra turned to check on the guards. "Joseph is watching us from the door," she told Alyssa.

"What's he doing?"

"He's talking to Henry and the other guy. They're shaking their heads."

She stood up and turned to look back. "Hmm, looks like Joseph is trying to talk them into something."

While they watched, the two guards nodded and with looks of fear, took a step outside onto the loading dock. They stood for a moment, looking around. Joseph said something and waved his hand to go on. The guards took a breath and walked across the dock and down the steps. Again they hesitated. It was clear they didn't want to step on the ground.

Joseph shouted something and the two men's shoulders hunched. They took the step.

"They coming out here," Kyra said.

"Looks like it. Are they going to guard us?"

"I don't know." Kyra unslung her bow and nocked an arrow.

Alyssa held out her hand. "Don't shoot them, Kyra."

Kyra stared at her friend. "Why not?"

The two watched the men take careful steps toward them. Fear and wonder was spread across their faces in equal measure. "Look at them! They're afraid but they're coming anyway. Joseph has them all knotted up inside."

"All the more reason to shoot them," Kyra said.

"No." Alyssa put her hand out again. "What will happen if you kill one or both of them? Our packs are inside. We won't be able to get away."

Kyra gripped and re-gripped the bow. She saw Henry and the other man stop and watch her. The wonder was gone; now there was just fear on their faces. "Fine." She slid the arrow back into her quiver and slung her bow over her shoulder. The men hurried toward them while Joseph stood in the door. Dan appeared beside him.

"Looks like we have an audience," Kyra nodded toward the building.

Henry spoke first when the two men arrived. "You both must come inside."

Alyssa pointed at the trees beside them, now a healthy green. "Look, these are hazelnut trees. They'll provide you with nuts, a good source of protein and fresh food for your community. They'll bloom next year, it's too late in the spring for it now. Then you'll have nuts to add to your food pantry."

Both of the guards stared. "I remember nuts from when I was little," Henry said.

"You can have them again if you let me keep healing the area around your community," Alyssa told him.

He pulled his eyes away from the trees and back to the young women. "Right now you must come inside."

Kyra sighed. "Fine. I need to wash Alyssa's hands first."

He waved for her to go ahead. After the hand wash, the young women walked back to the warehouse door, Henry and the other guard close behind them. When they got there, Dan was waiting. "You need to go to your room," he said. He turned and they followed. Kyra dragged Alyssa into the washroom as they passed by it.

The guards shouted as they went in. Kyra shut the door in their faces. "We need to use the facility," she yelled. "Quick, Alyssa." She pulled her water bottle off and gave it to her friend. "Fill these up. Who knows how long they'll keep us in the room," she whispered.

A fist banged on the door. "Come out of there," Dan said loudly. "Right now."

"As soon as we're finished," Kyra said, her back to the door. "Use the bucket, too."

Alyssa nodded and did as she was told. She replaced Kyra at the door and Kyra used the bucket, too. She re-adjusted her clothing and called out. "We're coming out." When they opened the door, Henry and the other guard were against the opposite wall, and Dan stood in the doorway. His fists were clenched and his brown eyes shot fire. "Don't ever do that again."

He waved the women on and followed them to their room. "You'll stay here until you're called," he said as they went inside.

Kyra turned to the door. "When will that be?"

"When Joseph says so." He closed the door. The two women could hear it lock from the outside. They stared at the door; a thin band of dim light shone across the bottom of the door. The lamp had not been lit.

"Huh," Kyra said as she groped through the dark to the end of her bed. "That went well."

Alyssa was still at the door. "What are you doing?"

"Getting my fire starter. I'll get the lamp going in a bit, stay where you are."

Soon Kyra found her starter by feel and crept to the lamp. She didn't want to knock it over in the dark. It took only a minute and the lamp was lit. Alyssa walked to her bed and sat down, hands in her lap. "You still have those rations?"

"Yeah." Kyra pulled a dried bean cake from her pocket. "Eat this and rest. I'm going to take a nap, too. Who knows how long they'll keep us in here."

JUDGEMENT

Kyra dragged the small table holding the oil lamp to the end of her bed when she woke from her nap and lit it again. She had read the book she took from the school library and left it at the department store at their last resupply and picked up a new one. She was reading it aloud to Alyssa, still lying on her bed, when they heard the key in the lock of their door. Kyra put a scrap of paper in her place and put the book under her pillow.

When the door opened, the two were sitting up, backs against the walls, looking at Henry, who had opened the door. "You must come with me." Kyra shrugged and slid off of the bed. Alyssa followed. Henry led the procession, Kyra and Alyssa in the middle, and two different men following behind. They took a path through the corridors new to Kyra. A glance at the windows showed it was dark outside. They arrived in a different warehouse space, this one decorated as a church. Kyra was familiar with the chapel at school. It was a simple, calm spot to sit and think, despite the statue of Jesus on the cross hanging at the front of the room.

This room was decorated in red. Red curtains were hung to make walls along both sides. Chairs had been brought and lined up in rows on both sides of a central aisle. Every chair had an occupant. Kyra spotted Barbara on the far left, in the back row. She looked scared. At the front there was a stage, about three feet off of the floor, painted in white; steps about five feet wide led up to the stage in the center. Joseph was on the stage, Dan behind him and to Joseph's right. The community was quiet, even the children who were seated with their parents. The two guards dropped away when they entered the church. Henry led them to the bottom of the stairs and peeled off to the right.

Kyra glared up at Joseph. Before she could speak, Joseph started. "Beloved of our Lord God. We have prayed and prayed. What to do, Dear Lord? What to do?"

Kyra rolled her eyes. This guy was insane. The community behind her was silent. *Surely these people aren't buying all of this crap?*

"Then the Lord answered my prayer," his baritone echoed off of the hard ceiling overhead. The crowd called out, "Amen!"

"The thought sprang into my mind that the girl, Alyssa, is here in answer to our prayers."

"Amen!"

"She's cleaning the filth of the betrayers, the evil Government, the blasphemers, the sodomites, the adulterers!"

"Amen."

He strode up and down the stage in front of Kyra and Alyssa, his arms waving. Sweat began to form on his face. "What we have here is a sin-eater!" He thrust his arm out from the center of the stage at Alyssa.

"Hallelujah!" the crowd shouted.

"This child is from God! Can you deny it? Look at her hair, her skin! Isn't this the very picture of an angel?"

The congregation chorused his words. "An angel, an angel!"

Kyra glanced at Alyssa, who shrugged. Neither of them had much use for religion. They listened politely on Sunday when the Mother Superior of the school stood in the chapel to talk about the blessings of God, but they both considered the Mother a little daft, though very kind.

"Look how she heals the land. Soon we'll be able to go outside, grow more food, and refresh our souls with the pure sunlight of God."

Now some of the men as well as the women were weeping aloud. "Bless you, Jesus! Bless you, Jesus!"

"I now declare, Alyssa is our sin-eater! No one may harm her in anyway. Virgin she is and virgin she shall remain. She will lay with no man upon pain of death for that man. She will stay with us forever and ever and heal the land for the Community of the Children of God. This is a sign that we are the righteous of this sinful world."

The crowd cheered. Kyra and Alyssa turned to look at the frenzy. Ruth and Glenna in the first row were weeping uncontrollably. To Kyra's eyes, Jessica looked jealous. There was no way to see Barbara off in the back. Men and women were leaping up and down in place with joy, tears streaking down their faces.

"Still!" Joseph shouted over the noise. The crowd quieted. "We still have one other to consider. This caused even more prayer. The child, Kyra, is willful, disobedient, and anti-social. What, dear Lord, should we do with Kyra?"

The community sat down into their chairs and leaned forward. Kyra turned back to the preacher. "How do I proceed, dear Lord?" Joseph stopped striding back and forth and pointed at the crowd. "What do I do?" He flung his hands wide. "The Lord has not seen fit to tell me."

The congregation moaned. *Really?* Kyra turned to look at them again. *They actually look sad!*

"I must pray more, dear ones of Christ." Joseph dropped his arms to his sides and hung his head. He shook it with sadness. "I have not received instruction, not yet." He looked up at the group. "For now, the two will be housed together, as they came together. But Kyra will not be allowed the freedom of the community. She will not be allowed to contaminate our innocent children, our daughters and sons, with her wicked willfulness, disobedience, and disrespect."

Mutters arose from the crowd. "Good thinking." "Well done." "That's right." echoed around the space. Kyra's heart beat hard and her stomach was in such a knot she was glad it was empty. Alyssa took her friend's hand.

"She will remain in her room, until the Lord sends me the righteous way." He flung his hands into the air while Henry and the two other guards surrounded the two young women. "Let us sing!"

As the guards led them away, the congregation broke into a rousing chorus of 'Onward Christian Soldiers.'

THEY FIND A FRIEND

The next morning Henry and the other guards opened the door. "Time for breakfast," he said, stone-faced. Alyssa and Kyra were already awake and dressed. The lamp had run out of oil last night and it was impossible to tell whether it was day or night in the windowless room. They got up from Kyra's bed where they had sat together, backs against the wall. Henry escorted them to Dan's table and stood behind them when they sat down. This morning, when one of the men began to pray, Kyra realized the men took that responsibility in turn. Before she and Alyssa could react, Henry and the second guard grabbed their hands and jerked them up over their heads. When Kyra tried to take her hands down, he held them in the air, her arms stretched until she thought her arms would pop out of their sockets. After prayer, he dropped them but didn't move.

Dan stared at them as Ruth deposited bowls of oatmeal in front of them. "You will follow the teachings of the community. No more anti-social behavior. You will do as you are told." He looked specifically at Kyra. "You will be respectful to the leaders of the community. Speak when spoken to, answer directly and keep your eyes down." He pointed his finger at Kyra. "No more challenges to my authority. Challenges to authority, disrespect, willful behavior, anti-social behavior are punishable by banishment."

He glanced at his teenage son. "Andrew, what is banishment?"

The teen stopped with his spoon halfway to his mouth. He put it back in the bowl. "Banishment is the punishment for a person who refuses to live by the tenants of the community. The person is escorted to the warehouse door and shoved out onto the loading dock with nothing but the clothing on their backs. The door is closed to them." He swallowed. "Forever."

"You shove people out into a toxic environment?" Kyra's voice was incredulous.

Henry cuffed her in the head. Knocked almost off of her chair, Kyra spun around, hand to her head, eyes watering with the pain of the slap. She'd never been hit in her entire life except in martial arts or by accident. The concept hurt more than the cuff. She turned and stared wide-eyed at Dan.

"Women and children do not speak at the table unless spoken to."

She looked along the table. Ruth and all of the kids had their eyes firmly on their food.

"That is a reminder. You will eat now." He picked up his spoon and dug into the oatmeal.

Kyra took her hand from her head and picked up her spoon. She noticed her oatmeal wasn't as watered down as yesterday, but it was still thin. A look at Alyssa's bowl showed a normal portion. She was glad at least for that. With all of the healing, Kyra wasn't sure how much longer her friend could go on without sufficient food. She finished her thin breakfast just before Dan.

"Get up," Henry told her and Alyssa.

The two rose from their seats. Ruth and Jessica gathered the breakfast bowls. "Come with me," Henry told them.

Kyra was surprised to find they were going back to the room. The door was already open. When they went in, a man was in there, stuffing their things into their packs.

"What are you doing?" Kyra cried out. She took a step toward the man with their things.

Henry grabbed her arm and held her. "We are taking these things from you. They've been deemed unclean. You will receive belongings from the community."

The man in the room finished with the packs and grabbed her bow and quiver. When he finished, he passed by them and left the room. Alyssa looked calm, even though she was being held, too. Kyra tried to free her arm from Henry's grip.

"Just a minute," he said. That's when one of the other guards stepped around them and deftly removed the knife from her boot. He did the same with Alyssa.

"No!" Kyra shouted.

Henry shook her arm. "Calm down. You have no need for weapons in the Community." He released Kyra with a little shove. "Get Alyssa's water bottles."

It took her a moment to process the request. When she looked around, she realized that the water bottles were right where they had left them. She walked over to the end of Alyssa's bed and picked them up. Henry held out his hand. "She'll need them outside today."

Kyra handed them over. At least that much was going right.

The man holding Alyssa pulled her to the door and out. Henry backed out of the room and grabbed the door knob. "You will stay here."

Kyra watched, dumbfounded, as he closed the door and locked it. She ran over and pounded on it. "Let me out! I have to protect her!" The pounding went on for several minutes but no one responded. As her eyes adjusted she realized light came in through a crack under the door. She lay flat on the cold cement floor and with one eye looked into the hallway. She couldn't see anything but the dirty hallway floor and the base of the opposite wall. Tears of frustration leaked from her eyes.

I'm supposed to protect her, she wallowed in her misery. *How can I do that locked up in here?* She sobbed quietly for a few minutes, then wiped her eyes and got up off of the cold floor.

The hours dragged by. Kyra could hear people passing in the corridor outside as she exercised. Squats, lunges, push-ups, and running in place helped but still it seemed like an eternity before Alyssa was escorted into the room. Henry filled and lit the lamp. Apparently, at least, Alyssa deserved light. They hugged fiercely.

Alyssa cupped Kyra's face. "How are you?"

Kyra wiped her eyes and a blush betrayed her emotions. "I'm fine. They kept me in here all day, in the dark."

Alyssa hugged her again. "I'm so sorry. Maybe I can tell them to let you come with me."

"Don't bother." Kyra slung her braid from her shoulder to her back. "They want to break me." She studied her friend. "Did you know that Malcolm was a soldier, back in his youth? He told me about how he was captured and kept in a dark room, tortured."

"Oh no!" Alyssa's eyes went wide.

"He said he was only telling me because of our trip. He wanted to prepare me. At least I'm not being tortured."

Alyssa took Kyra's hands and looked into her friend's gray-blue eyes. "But you are being tortured. Maybe the worse kind for you, being kept in a small room, in the dark." She hugged her friend again.

Kyra accepted the hug then broke away. She wiped her eyes again. "What happened with you?"

"They chained my ankles together." She pulled up her pant legs. Her ankles were chafed red.

"The bastards!" Kyra knelt down to look. "How are your feet? What did they use?"

"Chains," Alyssa said as she walked over to her bed and sat down. "I had plenty of chain to take my normal steps but the chain between my feet kept catching on things, breaking my rhythm." She scrubbed her face with her hands and pulled her hair off of her sweaty face. "I'm more tired today than I was the first day of our trip."

Kyra sat beside her on the bed and put an arm around Alyssa's shoulders. She gave her a squeeze. "I'm so sorry, Alyssa. Malcolm told me there would be weird survivor communities; I just couldn't imagine any place that didn't behave like ours. As much as I chafed there, now I appreciate how well balanced our home was."

The two young women held hands. "Nothing we can do about this now."

They sat silent for a few minutes. Kyra spent the time mentally kicking herself for getting Alyssa into this mess, forgetting that it was Alyssa who was determined to go out into the world. "What do we do now? How can we get out of here?"

"I have no idea. They had two guards on me all day. It was all I could do to relieve myself with any privacy. The chains on my feet make it impossible to run, even if I would leave you behind."

Kyra nodded. "Maybe…"

The sound of the door unlocking made her stop and turn. Henry opened the door. They could see there was another guard against the facing wall. Henry stepped aside and Barbara came in with a tray. Henry shut the door.

She stood a moment, looking both sad and confused. "They sent you dinner. I'm really sorry," she said as she held the tray. "Alyssa gets the full bowl. Kyra, I have to give you the broth."

The two got up from the bed and walked over to the girl standing in the middle of the room. "Not your fault, Barbara," Kyra took the bowl meant for her as Alyssa retrieved hers. "Are you getting enough to eat?"

She nodded. "I'm off the hook, now that Alyssa has been named sin-eater. Joseph held a special ceremony and did a cleansing on me after you were taken away. In a few months I'll be sixteen and marriageable." She didn't look happy about it.

"Is that bad?" Kyra asked, her food still untouched.

"Yeah. There are more men than women. Since I have no parents, Joseph will be selling me off to the highest bidder among the unmarried men."

Kyra's eyes went wide. "You don't have a choice?"

The girl shook her head. "No woman has a choice. Joseph is the arbiter of all marriages. Women marry who he tells them to marry. Some of the men are all right. They treat their wives and children well. Others beat their wives for the least thing. It seems that the higher status the man has, the more likely they are to be wife-beaters. All of the highest-ranking men get wives, so maybe that's a good thing."

"I'm so sorry," Alyssa told her. She reached out to touch Barbara's hair. The girl flinched. "I beg your pardon, Barbara. Your hair looks so nice."

It did look nice. The girl's dark brown hair had been washed and combed out and fell down her back in long, brown waves. "Yeah. Now that I'm not the scapegoat, the women were ordered to clean me up. I still do all of the scut work but the beatings have mostly stopped."She sighed. "Anyway. While you eat I get to empty your bucket."

The two nodded and the girl got the bucket and went to the door. When she knocked, it opened and she left. They could hear the door lock again. Kyra and Alyssa sat down to eat. Alyssa transferred a few of the vegetables from her bowl to Kyra's despite her friend's protests."

"You need the energy, Alyssa. Don't give me your food." She tried to move her bowl away.

"Nonsense. How are you going to get us out of here if you're shaking and weak with starvation?"

Kyra relented--her stomach was growling--but she stopped her friend at just a few vegetables. "Enough. If you fall over from weakness outside, who knows what these crazy people will do?"

The two friends ate side by side on Alyssa's bed. It didn't take long to finish the meager meal. "Did you say their garden is in bad shape?" Kyra asked.

"I healed all of the plants in the beds but they don't have near as many beds as we did and I think the light is too poor for good growth. They really need the outside gardens."

They stopped talking at the sound of the key in the lock. The door opened and Barbara came back with the empty clean bucket. She put it down in the spot she had retrieved it from.

"Can you get us drinking water and some water to wash with?" Kyra asked.

"That's next," Barbara said. "Where are your water bottles?"

Kyra collected them all and gave them to the girl.

"I'll be right back for the bowls," she told them.

It didn't take long. She brought a pan of water and the water bottles and a rag. "This is the best I could do." She put them down and collected the bowls. "I'll help you as much as I can but as the lowest-ranked person in the community, there's not much I can do."

Kyra and Alyssa each hugged the girl. "Thank you," Alyssa told her.

"Can you find out where they're storing our things?" Kyra asked.

Barbara's eyes went wide and she looked over her shoulder at the door. "I don't know," she whispered. "I can listen around. No one pays much attention to me."

"I appreciate it, Barbara."

The door swung open. "Get a move on, kid," Henry growled. "I ain't got all night."

"Yes, Henry." She ducked her head. "I was just getting the bowls." She hurried to the door.

Henry eyed the two young prisoners with suspicion. "Don't get no ideas." He shut the door and locked it.

Kyra sighed. "We're putting all of our hope on a girl that's been abused all her life."

Alyssa nodded. "Let's hope that means she doesn't have any loyalty to them."

KYRA'S PUT TO WORK

Kyra was kept locked away in the dark for five days while Alyssa was taken out and forced to heal the land around the factory. Time dragged by for her with nothing to do in a dark room. The third day their captors realized Alyssa knew all of the plants she was healing and the head gardener followed her around while she identified every food plant she came across. On day six after the now normal breakfast of thin gruel and Alyssa being taken away, Kyra was shackled and taken to the kitchen. She was so hungry that her stomach hurt but she still refused Alyssa's food. She had a headache and dizzy spells, too, that she neglected to tell her friend about.

Ruth put her to work scrubbing pots, the kitchen floor, and the dining room floor. She emptied the vegetable scraps into the compost heap and collected the ranking member's night soil buckets to empty, clean and return to their proper places. She wasn't allowed to go anywhere outside of the kitchen or dining area alone. One of the guards always went with her.

One of the benefits of the menial work was that she grew to know the factory layout. She memorized every twist and turn in the makeshift corridors. Joseph's accommodations were a marvel. She had learned the word opulence in the school classrooms but other than pictures in books had never actually seen anything opulent. His room was the definition. Oriental rugs covered the cement floor. Wood paneling covered the walls and actual painted art hung around the room. There were several oil lamps, all cleaned and ready to light. Books lined the walls, though when she caught a quick look at the titles, was disappointed. They were all religious texts. Stuffed armchairs and sofas were in the room in conversational groups with low tables in the middle. The room itself was the size of one of the classrooms from home. *How do the rest let him get away with this?* She knew that even Dan's quarters, the second in the hierarchy, were only a quarter this size and plainly furnished.

Some days Barbara was set to scrubbing floors with Kyra. They whispered between themselves when no one was looking. Four days after Kyra was put to work, Barbara reported, "I've found your things. They're in Joseph's private store room."

"Where's that?" Kyra whispered.

"Down the hall from his apartment, three doors down, on the left. It's always locked."

"Is there anyone else who might help us, Barbara? It can't be that everyone is happy with this set up."

The two scrubbed harder as two women from the kitchen walked by. After they passed, Barbara said, "There's a few. One woman, married to a high-ranking guy, has always been nice to me. A few of the lowest-ranked men and teens are friendly, too. But I don't know if they'd help." She looked around the dining area when she heard voices in the kitchen.

"I heard Joseph the other day when I was told to clean the hall outside his office," Kyra whispered. "He may have a husband for you."

Barbara froze; her brown eyes searched Kyra's face. "Did you hear a name?"

"Davin, I think he said. He was talking to Dan. Dan thought the guy wasn't faithful enough but Joseph said that Davin was the next ranking man. It was his turn for a wife."

The girl slumped. "The guy's a jerk. He knocks over my mop bucket all the time. Him and his friends laugh while I have to clean up the mess."

Kyra put an arm around her. "I'm sorry, Barbara."

The girl began to scrub the floor as though she could grind a hole in it. "That's all right. At least Jessica won't have to marry him. She's always nice to me. It's too bad her father is such a pain."

Kyra resumed scrubbing. When they finished inching their way across the floor, she dropped the brush in the bucket. "I'm getting my arm workouts, anyway," she joked. Then she tried to stand. Her head swam and the room seemed to spin around her. Barbara caught her as she swayed and guided her to a chair.

"Are you all right?" she asked.

Kyra put her head between her knees. "Not enough to eat," she told the girl. "Thin gruel in the morning and broth at night with working all day at hard labor isn't cutting it. I'm so hungry," she confessed.

"I'll see if I can slip you some more food," Barbara told her.

Just then Glenna came into the dining room and saw the two together. She strode over to where Kyra was sitting as Barbara hovered over her. "What are you doing?" she yelled across the room.

Skin pale and sweating, Kyra looked up as the woman charged toward them. Barbara spun around, eyes wide.

"She nearly fainted," Barbara said in a hurry, eyes on the floor.

Kyra stared the woman down. "She helped me to a chair before I collapsed."

Glenna put both hands on her hips. She eyed the buckets next to the two. "Is this floor finished?"

"Yes, ma'am," Barbara whispered.

"I'm going to tell Ruth," she said. "Extra work for both of you and no dinner tonight."

"But--" Barbara began.

"Shut it!" Glenna pointed a finger at the girl. "Don't make me tell Joseph you were disrespectful."

Barbara's head drooped.

"Another incident of the two of you chatting and I'll report you." She stalked off to the kitchen.

Barbara's eyes filled with tears that ran down her face.

"What does that mean, she'll tell Joseph?" Kyra asked.

"Disrespect gets a flogging," Barbara said. She helped Kyra stand and pushed the chair back under the table.

"Flogging! You mean hitting you?" Kyra bent over and grabbed her bucket handle. She carefully stood up.

"With a whip, stripped bare to the waist, tied to a big wooden cross, like an X, that they raise in the sanctuary. Everyone has to attend." Barbara picked up the other bucket and the two walked to the industrial sinks where they dumped the buckets and rinsed them out.

Kyra realized how much danger Barbara was in, just to help them.

"I'm sorry I got you in so much trouble."

Barbara sighed. "Won't be the first time. Anything goes wrong, it's my fault. If the soup scorches, if a baby gets sick, it's all my fault. I get the beating."

Ruth stormed out of the kitchen and to the two young women. "Barbara, get over to the garden, the compost needs to be turned. Kyra, get to the nursery, the diapers need washing."

Barbara ducked her head and hurried off. Kyra looked Ruth in the eye. "Shall I go alone?"

Ruth stared, then blushed. "Wait for Henry while you get in the kitchen and clean the wall behind the stove."

Kyra strolled to the kitchen, Ruth behind her, cursing her insolence. Kyra knew she'd pay for it but she couldn't help herself. It was too easy to fluster the woman.

That evening in their room, Kyra told Alyssa about the incident.

"You shouldn't do that, Kyra," Alyssa said as they ate. "Think about how Ruth is getting beaten by Dan every day."

Kyra ran her finger around the bowl to get every bit of food out. She licked her finger, grateful the threat of no dinner didn't materialize. She felt like a scum for taunting Ruth. She remembered how sorry she'd felt for Ruth the first day. "She knows what it's like, why doesn't she treat others better?"

Alyssa's eyes were full of sorrow. "You know better. How well are you doing and you haven't been conditioned by years of abuse?"

That question made Kyra feel worse. "Yeah," she said defensively. "I guess."

Alyssa changed the subject. "Good news about where our things are. Any chance we can get to them and get out?"

Kyra took Alyssa's empty bowl and stacked it in hers. "I don't know. I'm not left alone anywhere outside of the kitchen or dining room. Maybe Barbara can convince some of the people she mentioned to help us."

Alyssa crossed her right ankle over her left knee. The ankle was raw. Spots of red, where the skin was worn away, showed as ugly blotches.

"Crap, Alyssa. They're going to be bleeding tomorrow."

"I know," she sighed. "It's hard to walk, the chafing burns so much."

"Maybe you can ask the guards not to chain you?"

She sighed. "I'll show them my ankles in the morning and ask." Alyssa put her foot on the floor and looked at her friend. "You're too thin. I don't like that you had a fainting spell this afternoon."

Kyra shrugged. "Barbara said she'd try to slip me some more food. I don't know where she's going to get it. She hardly gets any more than you do."

The door rattled and Henry let Barbara into the room. She had a bucket of water for washing and put it on the floor. She picked up the slop bucket. No one said anything as Henry held the door open. She gave them a quick smile before she took the bucket out. The door locked behind her.

"I'll bet they won't let us talk in here with her anymore," Kyra said.

They waited. When Barbara came back, she took their water bottles. On the return trip, she gathered up the bowls. Each time Henry held the door open and watched. On the last trip Barbara gave them an almost imperceptible shrug and left the room. Henry shut the door and locked it.

Kyra sighed. "Well, that's one chance at getting information gone. Let's hope they let us work together tomorrow."

Alyssa nodded. "I hope so. She's our only source of information."

KYRA'S UP FOR BID

After that, Kyra and Barbara had to be careful. Ruth made sure the two didn't work together. If they were on the same job, such as scrubbing the dining room floor, she made sure they were at opposite ends of the room. Barbara whispered to Kyra as they passed each other in the hallway, the kitchen or the nursery. Tiny bits of food passed hand to hand or were left in places Ruth wouldn't think to look. Three days later, the guards stopped escorting Kyra around. Joseph had decreed that it was unnecessary, so she was left in peace at least when she was moving from one spot in the factory to another. In the kitchen, as Kyra was collecting the scraps for the compost, Barbara whispered, "I have two friends to help us."

Kyra nodded that she heard and took the bucket of scraps to the compost. It was the best news she'd heard in two days. Ruth had been quick to bring out the "rod of discipline" as she called it and beat Kyra with the thin, whip-like stick for any infraction of the rules, real or imagined. It seemed to Kyra that Glenna was always nearby when these episodes occurred so she blamed Joseph's wife more than Ruth.

Ruth was another issue altogether. She always sported a black eye, bruises on her arms or legs, or winced, holding her ribs when she walked. None of the other women in the kitchen ever said a word about it but Kyra could see that they knew what was going on. They treated Ruth gently and with compassion. Kyra thought that in Ruth's place, that treatment would drive her crazy, but there was nothing she could do to help. Fortunately, Dan never came into the kitchen or dining area for anything but meals. There was that tiny thing to be thankful for at least.

That afternoon after scrubbing the nursery room floor, Kyra was carrying the heavy bucket of water to the utility sink when Barbara walked by. No one else was in the hall so she stopped. "One of our new friends is a guy just promoted to the Holy Guards. He hates the way things are going around here. All the best food and comforts go to Joseph and Glenna, then his elite, then the rest of us. The wife beating has really reached a point where many of the men are uncomfortable. You know how Ruth looks all the time. The whole community can see that."

Kyra nodded while constantly checking the hallway. She put the bucket down; it was hurting her hand.

"Anyway, he promised to get your stuff out of Joseph's storage when the time comes."

"Soon, I hope," Kyra said as she rubbed her hands together.

"It will have to be." Barbara looked up and down the hallway and lowered her voice. "Joseph has opened bidding on you."

"What?" She stopped rubbing the sore spot on her palm.

Barbara nodded. "It started this morning. He calls it a dowry."

Panic flooded her system. She didn't want to be trapped here, wife to someone she didn't even know. "It's not a dowry, I'm being sold. We have to get out of here. How long does this process take?"

"Joseph set a high price on you. Says you bring new blood into the community. It may take a few days." She reached out and touched Kyra's shoulder. "I'm sorry, Kyra." Her brown eyes were full of compassion.

Kyra tried to pull herself together. She chided herself for being an object of pity to a girl six years younger than she was and in the same boat to boot. She took a breath and tried to stop the little voice that was in the back of her mind, screaming. "I'm fine. Alyssa and I just need to get out of here. Let's set up the escape for tomorrow night."

Barbara's eyes narrowed. "That doesn't give me much time to hoard food for you."

"It doesn't matter." Kyra picked up the bucket. "They're starving me to death here anyway. I might as well starve out in the woods, free."

THE ESCAPE

Kyra spent the rest of the day doing her best to fill her pockets with whatever food she could find. She also collected a sharp knife, twenty feet of rope which she wound around her waist to hide, and a few rags. She didn't know what she was going to do with the rags but she took them anyway. The cleanest one she used to tie around her hair.

When Ruth passed by Kyra scrubbing vegetables, she stopped. "You covered your head."

Kyra paused, water dripping down her hands into the bowl where the carrots were soaking. "Yeah, my braid was falling into everything, now it stays on my back."

Ruth stared a moment, then grunted and walked on. She breathed a sigh of relief and finished the carrots. She pulled a half-eaten one out of her pocket and ate it tiny nibbles while no one was watching.

At dinner Kyra and Alyssa went through the motions of the meal prayer, ate quickly and waited for Dan to finish. Kyra thought she'd burst before they were put in their room and the door locked. Alyssa didn't look well. Her face was too thin and she hardly spoke.

"Are you all right?" Kyra asked as she sat on the bed beside her friend.

"I don't remember ever being so tired. They hardly let me rest. At least they took the chains off today." She shook her head. "Joseph actually came out to the field I was healing. Dan was pointing out all of the fruit and nut trees, talking about how the ground could be tilled, acting the bigshot. Joseph came over to me to say something but when he saw my ankles he was furious. The chains had rubbed them raw to the point of bleeding. It was running down my feet. "

"'How is this happening to our sin-eater?' he yelled at them." Alyssa lowered her voice in imitation. "He pointed at my feet. 'She's barefoot and bleeding. Is this how you treat God's gift to us?'" Alyssa lay back on the bed with a sigh. "Henry was out there. Joseph pointed at Henry and yelled at him, 'Get those off of her, right now!' I had to laugh. It's too late. My ankles will carry those scars forever, now."

Kyra patted her friend's leg. "I'm so sorry, Alyssa. But, I have news that may cheer you up."

Alyssa sat up. A spark of interest lit up her green eyes. "Tell me."

Kyra grinned. "We're getting out of here tomorrow."

"Really? How?"

"Barbara has made us a couple of friends. One is a guard. Holy Guards, is what Joseph calls them." She rolled her eyes and waved her hand. "Anyway, he's going to get our packs out of Joseph's store room. I've been hiding a little food and other things that could be helpful and Barbara has been hiding food for us, too."

Alyssa grabbed Kyra's hands. "This is the best news I've had in a long time."

"I know," Kyra said. "I also think that our arrival here has stirred things up. Barbara said there's a lot of discontent about how Joseph and Glenna live high on the hog and the rest of them suffer. It also seems that not all of the men like this culture of wife beating. The guard that's helping us falls into that camp."

Alyssa closed her eyes and nodded. "There's a lot of sadness here, a lot of fear and grief and despair and hatred." She opened her eyes. "I can feel it. It weighs me down until it seems as though I can't breathe."

Kyra hugged her. "I can feel it, too. And you know I'm emotionally thick as a brick."

The two began to giggle at the joke. They laughed until they cried. "There," Alyssa said as she wiped her eyes. "A good laugh and a good cry to wash away the tension."

"True," Kyra hiccupped and the two began laughing again. It was the best sleep they'd had since they arrived.

The next morning Alyssa was taken out to the fields and Kyra was back in the kitchen. Barbara whispered as she passed, "It's on for tonight," as Kyra scrubbed out the oatmeal pot. She fidgeted as she scrubbed and she had to resist the urge to check the knife she'd stolen yesterday and hid in her boot under her pants leg. She also resisted the urge to swear at whoever had let the oatmeal burn in the bottom.

Her distraction lasted all day. Ruth switched her twice for slopping water out of the floor-washing bucket and for missing a whole patch of floor in the kitchen. Kyra stood and took the beatings as she kept the plan for the night's escape in front of her mind. At mid-day she was on her way to the garden area when Alyssa, followed by Henry and another guard came in through the warehouse door. Kyra tried to come by here as often as possible when Alyssa was out. She needed to see the outdoors for one thing. The other was the hope of catching a glimpse of her friend to see if she was all right.

Kyra stopped. "What's wrong?"

"Nothing," Henry told her. "It's going to rain, so we came in."

Kyra looked out the door. The wind was whipping the trees back and forth and the sky was nearly black. "Looks like a big storm."

The guards pulled the door down. "It'll clean the windows a bit anyway and let more light into the garden," Henry said. When the door was down he told Alyssa, "You can sit in the dining room or in your room, which shall it be?"

"Dining room," Alyssa said. "It's lighter there."

He turned to Kyra. "Don't you have somewhere to be?"

Kyra ducked her head and picked up the scrap bucket. "Yes. I'm on my way." She winked at Alyssa as she hurried off to the garden. When she came back they could hear the rain beating on the metal roof of the factory in the dining area. She stopped at the table where Alyssa sat. Her friend's eyes were closed in a nap. Kyra made a little noise and her friend's eyes flew open. "Hey."

"Hey, yourself. Rest up. This storm will help us get out of here."

"Really? I thought we'd cancel because of the weather." She looked up into Kyra's face.

"Exactly. If we don't want to be out in the weather, neither will the guards, and they have less reason to be out there. So, tonight is on." She turned at the sound of the kitchen door swinging open. "I've gotta go." She hurried off as Ruth glared at Alyssa sitting at the table. By then Kyra was over at the utility sink rinsing out the bucket. Ruth went back into the kitchen.

The rest of the day dragged for Kyra. She jumped at every noise and constantly looked over her shoulder. She only saw Barbara once that afternoon, just before supper. There was no time to talk, she nodded and went on with her tasks.

At dinner Kyra kept her eyes on her bowl. She was afraid that if she looked at Dan she'd tell everything. After dinner he said, "It's good to see you and Alyssa fitting in, Kyra. That's the behavior that will make you a welcome addition to the community."

Kyra had to bite her tongue but she refrained from making a sarcastic comment. In their room, the door locked, Alyssa patted her on the shoulder. "I know how hard that was for you."

"Too hard. I wanted to fly over that table and smack him in the head." Kyra paced up and down in the room.

"When will we get out of here?" Alyssa asked.

"After everyone goes to sleep," Kyra said. "We should be lying down, resting, but I'm too keyed up."

"I've been sitting all afternoon," Alyssa chuckled. "But I'm going to lie down and rest. I'm so tired." She lay down on the bed and curled up on her left side.

Kyra turned down the lamp and lay down but didn't take off her boots. She wanted to be ready to go as soon as the door opened.

She jolted awake at the noise of a key in the lock. Kyra sat up and stared at the door in the dim light. When it opened, it was Barbara and her new guard friend. "Alyssa," Kyra called softly. "Time to go."

Alyssa got up and shoved her feet into her boots sockless. "I'm ready."

They picked up their full water bottles and hurried to the door. Barbara whispered, "This is Tom."

"Hi, Tom," Kyra said to the tall, blond man hulking in the doorway. "Thank you for helping us get out of here."

He handed them the packs. "I'm not sure if everything is there. Joseph may have removed things. I have no idea where your knives are."

"You did the best you could," she said as she shrugged into the pack. "Show us the way out."

The four of them hurried along the hallways, their booted feet echoing. Kyra tried to look in all directions for danger as she cursed the noise of their clomping down the hall. They came to the front door where they had first entered the community.

"This door makes a lot of noise," she said as Tom began to unlock the padlock on the chained door.

He shook his head. "Joseph had us fix it. I just have to get the chains off quietly."

"Why are you doing this, Tom?" Alyssa asked.

Kyra was afraid he'd stop working but he answered as he carefully lifted the chain from the door push bars. "My dad never liked Joseph. When we first got here, Joseph was just a minister of some small, off-shoot Baptist church. He wasn't in charge, but, ministers, they're important people and the survivors went to him for comfort. After a few years he was in charge."

A chain link clanked against the metal door and everyone froze. Kyra held her breath at a noise down the hall. When nothing happened, Tom went back to work. "My dad, he didn't care too much one way or the other about Joseph, but a lot of the people here pushed him into power. Then there were all the new rules. Gradual at first and my dad, well, 'go along to get along' was his motto. It wasn't until about four years ago the crazy really started to come out, when Joseph was put in charge after our old leader died."

Barbara stepped to the door to help him manage the chain. Links clinked together and again, everyone froze. The rain had stopped and the metal roof popped as it cooled. Barbara and Tom continued to remove the chain. Kyra's heart was beating in her ears.

"What happened?" Alyssa asked.

"I don't know," Tom said. His blue eyes looked into her green ones. "All of a sudden he had a bunch of bully boys and the rest of us did as we were told." He stopped for a moment. "Anyone that objected was shoved out of the warehouse door into the brown sludge." His voice broke for a second. He cleared his throat. "My dad was one of them."

Kyra sucked in her breath at that revelation.

"I'm so sorry, Tom," Alyssa whispered.

He removed the last of the chain from the door and handed it to Barbara. "I think I was accepted into the Holy Guard because I'm big," he said as he put his hand on the push bar. "Anyway, let's get you out of here."

Tom pushed the bar and the door swung open with only a little squeak. Kyra started for the door, Alyssa on her heels. She stopped outside and looked at Barbara. "Aren't you coming?"

Barbara shook her head. "No. I'm staying here to help clean up this community. Now that you healed some land for us, Alyssa, I think we can make this a better place. Thank you for that."

Alyssa smiled. "You're welcome. Good luck."

They heard a shout from inside. "Tom! What are you doing?"

Kyra and Alyssa took off, Alyssa in the lead following the path she made coming into the community. Tom slammed the door shut. The last thing they could hear as they ran was the sound of the chain being wrapped around the door.

I hope they make it, Kyra thought as she ran.

The End

EXCERPT FROM BROWN RAIN: THE DOWNTRODDEN

Alyssa and Kyra ran as best they could through the dark. They didn't dare get off the path Alyssa had made weeks ago or Kyra would be poisoned. For awhile they could hear pursuers from the Community of the Children of God but it didn't last long. They were working with torches and the light was too dim for them to see a path they didn't even knew existed.

The run up the hill overlooking the town was hard; neither of the two young women had been fed well during their imprisonment. At the top, Kyra called for a stop. "Wait, Alyssa," she gasped, heart beating furiously. She felt as though she were going to vomit. "I haven't heard any noise behind us since two blocks away from the factory. I think we're safe."

Alyssa turned to look down the hill as she dragged in breath in great rasping sobs. The dim moonlight showed her hair stuck to her face. "I don't see any torches."

They were stopped in the spot where they had first looked over the town. Alyssa sat down, Kyra collapsed beside her. They both watched; there were no lights following them. "Can we sleep here?" Alyssa asked.

The two had stopped at the top of the ridge at the edge of the woods where they had stood many days before. "Can you make us a clearing?" Kyra asked. "I don't want to chance rolling into the brown rain."

Her friend swallowed and pulled hair that was stuck to her face back and into the rest of her hair. "Let me catch my breath," Alyssa said.

They sat for several minutes as their heart rates dropped and breathing went back to normal. Alyssa began healing the ground around them while she sat there, reaching out around her and clearing a space. "I'll do the best I can," she said. "It's too dark to see here under the trees."

"Big enough for us to lie down," Kyra told her. "I don't know what's in our packs. Joseph may have taken the tent and who knows what else. I won't know until I can look in the packs." She could feel Alyssa nod more than see her.

The teen got up and leaned over, creating a space under a large pine tree where they would have a little shelter, then she healed the tree. She sank down, back against the newly healed bark. "That's all I can do," she told her friend. "I'm just too tired and hungry."

"Good enough for me," Kyra told her as she stepped lightly to sit beside Alyssa. "This will do till daylight, then we have to move."

The next morning the sun woke them by shining through the branches of the tree. Kyra woke first to the smell of pine and sunlight in her eyes. She yawned and listened. There was no sound of pursuit. She nudged

Alyssa. "Get up. I want to go before Joseph convinces the men of the community to follow our path."

The two stood up, stretched and trotted along the path they'd previously made. "Where are we going?" Alyssa asked.

"I want to back track a bit then see what's in my pack. I hope the maps are still there and our tent, at least. The rest of the supplies would be a bonus but I suspect Joseph may have taken most of it. My pack feels too light."

They walked and jogged for about the time it took the sun to move another hand above the horizon. "How do you know that's an hour?" Alyssa asked when Kyra called a halt.

"It's a trick Malcolm showed me," Kyra said as she shrugged off the pack. You hold your hand horizontally above the horizon. Then move it up little finger where the thumb was until you reach the sun. If it's morning, that's how many hours it's been since sun rise. In the afternoon, that's how many hours until sunset." She shrugged as she knelt on the four foot wide path, next to a stream. "It's not totally accurate, like the old time clocks, but it's a fair measure."

Alyssa sat down to rest, careful to keep her hands to the edge of the path. "Do you have any water left?"

Kyra unslung one of the bottles they had filled before their escape. "A little; let me pour for you." She rose and walked over to her friend. She tipped the bottle to her mouth. "Drink as much as you want. If the pot is gone, I'll dip water with an empty bottle and you can clean that before I fill the rest."

Alyssa drank it all. "Thanks," she said as she wiped her mouth on her shoulder.

Kyra went back to the pack. "Let's see what that miserable excuse for a community leader left us."

She pulled out spare socks, a spare shirt and a packet of dried bean cake. "Hah," she cheered. She counted. "Ah, he tried one, didn't like it and left the rest," she grinned. "At least we have something to eat." A little lower in the pack was their tiny cooking pot. "Nice," she held it up. "We can cook and dip water."

Alyssa grinned. "That's something anyway."

She dug down to the bottom of the pack. Kyra was really hoping for the tent as they had to abandon their sleeping bags at the factory when they escaped. "Got it," she crowed triumphantly. She pulled it out and unfolded it as much as she could in the limited space. "It looks undamaged as far as I can tell. We'll be cold at night but we'll be out of the wet, at least until we get to a town where I can find supplies."

"How about the maps?" Alyssa asked. "I'd hate to have to just wander around in the woods till we stumble on a town."

Kyra reached into the pack and felt around the bottom. "Wait, yep," she smiled again. "He left the maps in the bottom. "Can you fill the bottles while I check the map? I want to move on as soon as we can. I still feel too close to the Children of God."

Alyssa nodded and got up. Kyra handed off all of the bottles and opened maps until she found the right one for this area. After Alyssa cleaned her hands, they split a dried bean cake. They rested about an hour and checked Alyssa's pack. Since she carried only her own things, most of them were still there. "Glad for that, at least," Kyra told her as they finished eating. She held the map out. "Look," she pointed at the map. "This is the town we just left. We want to go west. If we follow this stream till mid-day then head a little north, we'll come to Fern Springs. It looks like it was a good sized town. We should be able to find food and gear there." She plucked a blade of grass and held it first against the map key, then the map. "It may take five days or so."

"What if the Community of God cleaned it out years ago when cars still worked?" Alyssa asked as she stood up and brushed off her hands.

"I thought of that." Kyra put the map at the top of her pack. She'd repacked the rest of the gear before they ate. "We'll have to deal with it as best we can. Maybe they just hit the big stores and skipped the hiking and sporting goods stores. All I know is that it's the closest town and we need food and gear. We have to try."

Alyssa nodded. "I'll keep my eyes open for edible greens. We can stew the bean cakes and maybe dress them up a bit."

"Sounds like a plan." Krya put on her pack and adjusted the straps while Alyssa did the same. "Let's go."

The Downtrodden is due out the end of October, 2014.

ABOUT THE AUTHOR

Connie Cockrell began writing in response to a challenge from her daughter in October 2011 and has been hooked ever since. Her books run the gamut from SciFi and Fantasy to Contemporary to Halloween and Christmas stories. She's published six novels and three collections of short stories and has been included in three different anthologies. Connie continues to write about whatever comes into her head.

Enjoyed First Encounter? Sign up to be notified of my next book at my newsletter.

Discover other titles by Connie Cockrell at CreateSpace.com:
A Trio of Animal Tales at https://www.createspace.com/4203850
Recall: https://www.createspace.com/4270855
Halloween Tales: A Collection of Stories:
https://www.createspace.com/4270855
Christmas Tales: https://www.createspace.com/4530573 (Also available in Large Print)
Gulliver Station Stories: A New Start:
https://www.createspace.com/4649337 (Also available in Large Print)
Her books are available in print at most online retailers.

Her next book in the series, Brown Rain: The Downtrodden, will be out near the end of October, 2014. See the excerpt above.

If you'd like to know more, go to
http://www.conniesrandomthoughts.wordpress.com or
https://www.facebook.com/ConniesRandomThoughts or
http://twitter.com/conniecockrell.

Made in the USA
San Bernardino, CA
19 July 2015